Praise for the Wor

Intertwining fictional charact... .... p...p.....
ments in American history, Lois Walfrid Johnson creates novels certain to catch the attention of readers, and then leaves them wanting to read and learn more. Johnson does an incredible job of bringing us into the lives of the American people in 1857. These adventure-filled, educational books should be read by youth everywhere.

> —**BILL INGEBRIGTSEN**, Minnesota State Senator,
> former Douglas County Sheriff

Lois Walfrid Johnson writes stories kids love. When they were young, my daughters read her Freedom Seekers books and really enjoyed them. These are stories that not only entertain, but call children to conviction, courage, and Christ-centered living. I highly recommend Lois and these excellent books.

> —**RANDY ALCORN**, *New York Times* bestselling
> author of forty books including *Heaven*

I've used *Escape into the Night* in my classroom for many years and am thrilled to see the new Freedom Seekers edition coming out with study guides. My students have always enjoyed the well-developed characters and engaging storylines. As a teacher I have appreciated the historical accuracy and timeless spiritual truths.

> —**JOCELYN ANDERSON**, teacher,
> Our Redeemer's Christian School, Minot, ND

It's difficult to find a series of books written for a variety of age groups with both boys and girls and yet remain historically accurate. Mrs. Johnson has succeeded in doing so in the Freedom Seekers series. Set in a geographic area that runs north and south, she describes weather conditions and topographical features that impacted the daring adventures of the main characters, their clothing, and even their food.

While developing the character of Peter, Mrs. Johnson visited with students at the Illinois School for the Deaf, including students in my classroom. We compared and contrasted the life of Peter to their lives. After all, Peter could have stood in our classroom! Often a child becomes a lifelong reader, simply because they relate to a character in a book. My students related to Peter, not only because he was deaf, but because he had so much more in common with them.

—**KATHLEEN COOK**, teacher,
Illinois School for the Deaf, Jacksonville, IL

I want to thank you on behalf of my class and their families for your wonderful books. I teach a reading class at a homeschool co-op in Washington State. I can't count how many times the parents of my students have thanked me for the class and told me that their child never enjoyed reading like they do now. They have to hold their children back from reading ahead of the others! So many families who are not in my class have begun to read your books. We may have started an epidemic, and one that I am happy to be a part of!

I hope you have more books on the horizon. Your fans here in Gig Harbor, Washington, will be on the lookout for them!

—**MARYANN KING**, homeschool co-op teacher,
Washington State

Your books have encouraged me in trusting in God more and more. Your characters, especially Libby Norstad, Caleb Whitney, and Jordan Parker, sound just so realistic! I sometimes wish that they were real!!!!!! I like how you introduced a new character [Peter] in the fourth book. It kept the story even more exciting than it is!

—**S.**, young reader, Texas

After I read one of your books I often end up asking myself, *Would I have helped slaves or not?* I have come up with an answer. I would help them because all people are equal and have the right to be free in the sight of God.

—**C. B.**, young reader, Kentucky

We love how you incorporate biblical principles into your stories. When Caleb trusts God and Libby struggles in the same areas we do, it shows us that through God we can overcome every obstacle, because He is our light and our salvation.

—**C. FAMILY**, Ohio

MYSTERIOUS SIGNAL

FREEDOM 5 SEEKERS

MYSTERIOUS SIGNAL

LOIS WALFRID JOHNSON

MOODY PUBLISHERS
CHICAGO

© 2013, 1998
LOIS WALFRID JOHNSON

Previously published as The Riverboat Adventures Series

Scripture quotations are from the King James Version of the Bible.

Interior Design: Ragont Design
Side-wheeler illustration by Toni Auble
Map of Upper Mississippi by Meridian Mapping
Sign language chart courtesy of the Illinois School for the Deaf, Jacksonville
Cover Design: Brock Sharpe & Associates / Faceout Studio, Tim Green
Cover Illustration: Odessa Sawyer

978-0-8024-0720-7- Printed by Bethany Press in Bloomington, MN – 07/13

Library of Congress Cataloging-in-Publication Data
Johnson, Lois Walfrid.
   Mysterious Signal / by Lois Walfrid Johnson.
      p. cm. (The Freedom Seekers; #5)
   Summary: Libby finds comfort in God's love as she faces the dangers of trying to help a fugitive slave escape to freedom through the Underground Railroad.
   ISBN 978-0-8024-0720-7
   1. Underground railroad—Juvenile fiction. [1. Underground railroad—Fiction. 2. Fugitive slaves—Fiction. 3. Christian life—Fiction.] I. Title. II. Series: Johnson, Lois Walfrid. Freedom seekers; 5.
PZ7.J63255Myf   1997
[Fic]—dc21   97—33958   CIP
                                                                   AC

We hope you enjoy this book from River North Fiction by Moody Publishers. Our goal is to provide high-quality, thought-provoking books and products that connect truth to your real needs and challenges. For more information on other books and products written and produced from a biblical perspective, go to www.moodypublishers.com or write to:

River North Fiction
Imprint of Moody Publishers
820 N. LaSalle Boulevard
Chicago, IL 60610

1 3 5 7 9 10 8 6 4 2

Printed in the United States of America

To Elise Grace—
Thank you for being willing
to grow your gifts
in writing and music,
for running the distance,
and most of all, for being
a caring Freedom Seeker!

* * * * * * * *

Abraham Lincoln, John Jones, Allan Pinkerton, Jesse Fell, Harriet Bishop, John K. Van Doorn, Avery Turner, Asa Turner, Frederick Douglass, Lieutenant Robert E. Lee, and Captain Philip Suiter are historic characters who lived in the 1850s. All other characters are fictitious and spring with gratitude for life from the author's imagination. Any resemblance to persons living or dead is coincidental.

In the time in which this book is set,
African Americans were called Negro,
the Spanish word for black,
or colored people.

Native Americans were called *Indians*.

The city of North Bloomington, Illinois,
also known as the Junction,
is now named *Normal* after
the Illinois State Normal University.

Contents

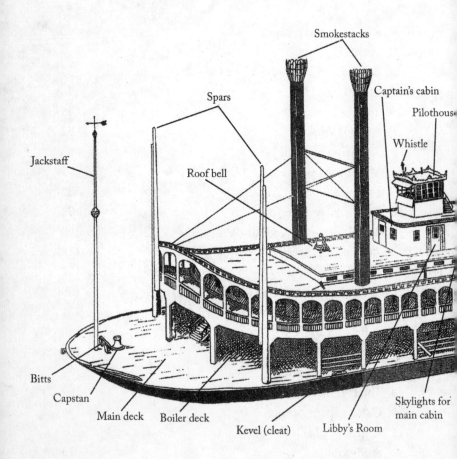

Smokestacks

Spars

Captain's cabin

Pilothouse

Jackstaff

Whistle

Roof bell

Bitts

Capstan

Main deck

Boiler deck

Kevel (cleat)

Libby's Room

Skylights for
main cabin

The Side-Wheeler
Christina

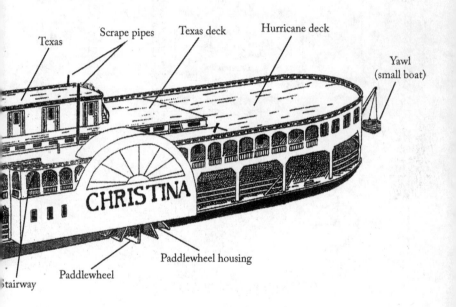

Texas

Scrape pipes

Texas deck

Hurricane deck

Yawl
(small boat)

CHRISTINA

Paddlewheel housing

Stairway

Paddlewheel

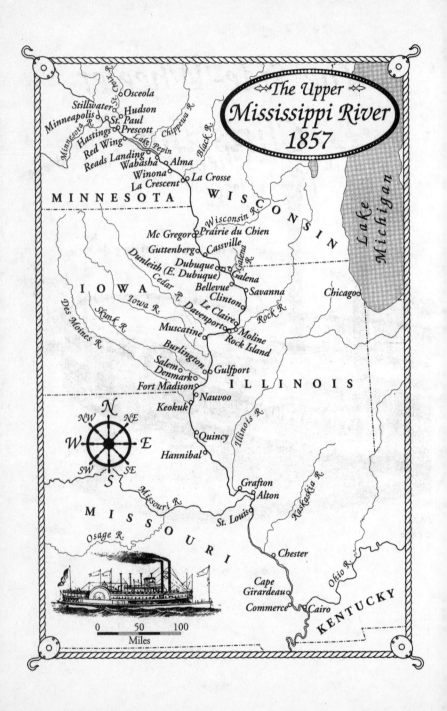

The Upper
Mississippi River
1857

MINNESOTA

WISCONSIN

IOWA

Lake Michigan

ILLINOIS

MISSOURI

KENTUCKY

St. Croix R.
Osceola
Stillwater
Minneapolis
Hudson
St. Paul
Prescott
Hastings
Red Wing
Reads Landing
Wabasha
Alma
Winona
La Crescent
La Crosse
Chippewa R.
Lake Pepin
Minnesota R.
Black R.

Wisconsin R.
Mc Gregor
Prairie du Chien
Guttenberg
Cassville
Dunleith (E. Dubuque)
Dubuque
Galena
Galena R.
Cedar R.
Bellevue
Clinton
Le Claire
Davenport
Iowa R.
Muscatine
Moline
Rock Island
Rock R.
Savanna
Chicago

Skunk R.
Des Moines R.

Burlington
Salem
Denmark
Gulfport
Fort Madison
Nauvoo
Keokuk
Illinois R.

Quincy
Hannibal

Grafton
Alton
Missouri R.
St. Louis
Kaskaskia R.
Osage R.
Chester
Cape Girardeau
Commerce
Cairo
Ohio R.

N
NW   NE
W   E
SW   SE
S

0   50   100
Miles

～ CHAPTER 1 ～

Run or Die!

Shhh!"

In the darkness of night the whisper came, a whisper so soft that at first Libby Norstad wondered if she had imagined it. Then on the night wind she heard it again.

"Shhh!"

A short distance ahead of Libby a thin, quick-moving man led the way—a free black who knew the hiding places well. From shadow to shadow he led the five of them. Using every patch of darkness—every bush, tree, wall, or fence—he protected them from curious eyes.

From her place near the end of the line, Libby counted. First their conductor—the man in the Underground Railroad who led fugitives from one safe place to the next. Then Jordan Parker, runaway slave. Behind him, Jordan's daddy, tall even in the shadows, and newly escaped. A marked man, Micah Parker was wanted by slave hunters for the reward he would bring. Next came ten-year-old Peter Christopherson, then Libby, and last of all, walking quietly behind her, Caleb Whitney.

Springfield, Libby thought. *Springfield, Illinois. Where can Jordan and his daddy be safe?*

"Walk when I walk," the conductor told them, his voice so low that Libby strained to hear. "Run when I run. Step only where I step."

For an instant Jordan turned, and the moonlight caught his face. In spite of the danger, his eyes seemed lit from within, showing his pleasure. He was with his father again!

Then Jordan faced forward and moved ahead without a sound. As one person, he and his father followed behind the man who led fugitives to freedom.

Suddenly a dog barked, filling the night air with fear. From nearby another dog answered with a deeper growl.

For an instant the Underground Railroad conductor paused. From one person to the next his whisper moved back. "Now or never. Run or die."

In the sliver of moonlight the conductor crouched. Under a row of bushes he went, and Jordan and his father followed. Behind them crept Peter Christopherson, youngest of all, yet full of courage. Ducking branches, Peter stayed low, keeping up with Jordan's daddy.

Then Libby, down on her hands and knees in the dirt. Under the hedge she crept through a hole in a fence. Out on the other side, she ran toward a dog that growled deep in his throat.

As Libby drew closer, the dog leaped out to the end of his leash. Filled with terror, Libby raced past. Already those in front of her were shadows, far ahead, fleeing for their lives. Running after them, Libby heard only the soft pad of Caleb's footsteps behind her.

Behind Caleb, the dog barked again. Now Libby knew him for what he was—a bloodhound trying to wake his owner.

Demanding that he be set free, the bloodhound was trained to track down runaway slaves, to keep them from reaching freedom.

A block farther on, a large barn loomed up in the darkness. For only a second the man in the lead paused. Then he pushed open a door—a yawning hole, dark and empty looking in the night. As their leader stood to one side, Jordan disappeared into the barn, followed by his father, Peter, Libby, and Caleb.

Inside was a deeper darkness. Waiting, Libby listened. So softly she almost missed it, the door closed behind them.

"Come," said the quiet voice.

No lights yet, no sound other than his voice. Then a hand took Libby's. As she grasped it, Libby felt Peter's tug and knew she had become part of a chain. Pulled forward in the darkness, they walked faster now, sure of the person at the head of the line.

Moments later they stopped.

"Wait," the man whispered. "Don't move."

With every sense alive Libby listened. From somewhere nearby she heard the snuffle of animals. Then a horse stamped his foot. Instead of seeing, Libby felt movement around her. *A livery stable?* she wondered. *A place for boarding or hiring out horses?* She felt sure it was.

Again a door closed. Another whisper, "Quiet! Be still!" The scratch of a match. Then the dim light of a kerosene lantern hanging from a nail on a huge beam.

Looking around, Libby saw that they were inside an inner room of the stable. Without being told, she knew that no light shone through the cracks to the outside windows. Along two walls were mounds of hay where people could rest. A pail of water with a tin cup waited nearby.

As Caleb joined the men, Libby sat down on the hay next to Peter. Her heart still pounding, Libby thought back to their race through the darkness.

Five months before, in March 1857, Jordan Parker had escaped from slavery. Then less than two weeks ago, Jordan's father, Micah, also escaped, fleeing across the Mississippi River to the free state of Illinois.

Free, Libby thought. *But not safe. Not even here in Springfield, the capital of Illinois.*

Because of fugitive slave laws, slave hunters could follow runaways into free states. There, slave catchers could gather a posse to capture and bring runaways back to their owners. Since his escape, Jordan's father had been hiding from men who wanted the big reward he would bring.

Less than an hour before, in the Springfield house that had offered shelter, Libby and her friends were wakened.

"We're being watched," said the woman who had taken them in. "Jordan and his daddy need to leave while they can." In the darkness of that second week in August, her husband had discovered a man standing across the street, tucked close to a barn, but not out of sight.

Fumbling in the dark to pull together her few belongings, Libby had dressed quickly. In the kitchen she found one candle lit. Heavy curtains hid its flame from the outside world.

Jordan and Micah Parker were already waiting. Along with Caleb and Peter, Libby listened to the free black man give instructions. As a conductor, he helped fugitives in the Underground Railroad reach freedom.

"So far there's only one man watching us," he said. "Soon there will be three or four or five, perhaps a mob. Someone will come with a search warrant. We'll sneak out on the other side of the house while we can."

His gaze steady, the Underground Railroad conductor searched their eyes to be sure they understood. "Do exactly what I do. You must be quiet. You must obey me instantly."

Libby glanced at Peter and held a finger across her lips to say "Shhh!" Peter nodded with understanding.

Moments later the conductor led them through the door on their race through the darkness. Now, only minutes after reaching the livery stable, that race seemed like a nightmare to Libby. Sitting on a pile of hay in the hidden room, she leaned forward to listen.

"You must leave Springfield right away," the free black man told Jordan and Micah. Heads bent, voices low, they stood in a huddle beneath the hanging lantern.

"Me and Daddy needs to go to Chicago," Jordan answered.

"Then I'll see that you two get to the Junction at North Bloomington," the man said. "Two railroad lines cross there. You can catch a train and be in Chicago in no time."

Though the Underground Railroad conductor meant a real train, fugitives more often walked or traveled by other ways. The words *Underground Railroad* described the secret way that escaped slaves passed from one place of shelter to the next. Often these stations were about twelve miles apart, a good distance for horses needing to make a trip and return home before dawn.

"We'll start now, and I'll take you as far as I can," the man said.

But Jordan looked concerned. "What about the money we found?" he asked Caleb.

Jordan's church in Galena, Illinois, had worked hard to raise money to help fugitive slaves get across Lake Michigan to Canada. Soon after the members asked Jordan to carry the money to Chicago, it was stolen. After a long search, Libby, Jordan, and Peter found it, along with money stolen from Libby's father. For safekeeping they had left it at the Springfield police station.

"I'll get the money," Caleb told Jordan.

"By wagon it takes me eight or nine hours if I don't have trouble changing horses," the conductor said. "If you take the morning train out of Springfield, you can meet Jordan and Micah in North Bloomington at about eleven o'clock. There's more than one depot at the Junction. Look for them in the freight room of the St. Louis, Alton, and Chicago Railroad."

"What if we need help?" Caleb asked. Since the age of nine, he had worked with Libby's father as an Underground Railroad conductor. Now fourteen, almost fifteen, Caleb was used to figuring out ways to help fugitives travel from one safe place to the next.

"I have a friend in the baggage room of the depot who will help you," the man answered. "If he's not there, look for a signal. Find a safe house on your own."

"A safe house?" Libby blurted out, even though she knew she should only listen.

"An Underground Railroad station. A place that hides fugitives until it's safe for them to go on."

Safe, Libby thought. Even the word sounded good.

"Move quickly now," the conductor said, his voice low. "Don't go close to the windows."

The door he touched swung open on oiled hinges. Taking the lantern with him, the conductor moved into the main part of the stable.

As Libby followed, she looked first for the windows. In spite of the well-kept appearance of the rest of the livery stable, the window glass was coated with a heavy layer of dirt, cobwebs, and bits of hay. Libby suspected that they had not been washed for years, probably for a good reason.

Staying low, Jordan and Micah Parker moved swiftly through the dimly lit area of the barn. Two strong, sleek horses were already hitched to a farm wagon. Libby had no doubt why they were chosen. When their long legs stretched out, they probably outdistanced any horse that tried to follow.

The wagon to which the horses were hitched was unlike anything Libby had ever seen. Jordan and Micah crawled into a false bottom beneath the usual boards in the wagon bed. Stretched out, they lay side by side in the small area.

The driver shut them in, then motioned for Libby, Caleb, and Peter to climb into the back of the wagon. When he clucked to the horses, they walked ahead, then stopped while the man shut the doors of the stable. Moments later he leaped up to the high seat, took the reins, and clucked again. The horses moved out in a slow walk that made less noise than a trot.

They had traveled only a short distance when Libby heard dogs bark again. As her heart leaped into her throat, Caleb shook his head and whispered, "Don't worry."

Just then Libby noticed Peter's expression. He sat without moving, staring into the night. He always watched closely, picking up even small facial expressions that helped him understand what was happening. Yet because Peter was deaf, he had not heard the dogs.

Does that make him less afraid? Libby wondered. Reaching out, she touched his hand and found it cold in spite of the warm night. Perhaps not hearing made scary things even more frightening. Libby pointed to the slate Peter carried in a bag over his shoulder, as though to promise, "I'll explain soon."

A short time later, the driver stopped the horses near some trees. "Do you know where you are?" he whispered.

On their knees, Libby, Caleb, and Peter looked over the high sides of the wagon. Down the block lay a depot with a large sign that said *Springfield*. Tracks ran along one side of the building, then disappeared into the darkness.

Again the Underground Railroad conductor whispered, "You're on your own now. The good Lord go with you."

Caleb stretched out his hand. "Thanks for everything."

When Libby, Caleb, and Peter jumped down from the end of the wagon, the driver barely lifted the reins and the horses responded. As the wagon rolled away, Caleb pointed to the trees. Without a sound he led them into the shadows, then stopped. When he leaned against a tree, his tall slender body seemed to blend with the bark.

To Libby it felt as if Caleb waited forever. As the hours stretched long, she grew more and more restless. But Caleb stood without moving. Libby had no doubt that he waited to be sure they brought no trouble on the Underground Railroad conductor and his family. Together they watched to see if anyone had followed them from the livery stable.

Following Caleb's lead, Peter stood next to him. With the

same blond hair and blue eyes, he looked like Caleb's younger brother.

Finally in the gray light before dawn, Caleb took Peter's slate. After losing his hearing through brain fever, Peter had learned sign language at the school for the deaf in Jacksonville, Illinois. Now Libby and Caleb were learning sign language from him. The slate helped them explain things they didn't know how to sign.

Using the shortcut words he and Peter had worked out between them, Caleb explained about Jordan and his daddy. Then he pointed to the depot and wrote, "Telegram. Libby's pa."

Along the street no one moved. In the half-light Libby heard only the twittering of birds. Then Caleb slung his knapsack onto his back, and Peter did the same.

"Let's go." For the first time all night, Caleb spoke aloud.

Just hearing his voice made Libby feel better. Anxious to get moving, she tossed her head and her long auburn hair swung about the knapsack on her back. Libby thought about what was inside—a change of clothes, needle and thread, sewing scissors, packets of food, drawing paper and pencils. *Am I ready for whatever lies ahead?*

Then Libby knew. *If I'm not, there's no turning back. No second chance.*

CHAPTER 2

Peter's Fear

Caleb, Libby, and Peter stepped out. Their watchfulness while racing through the darkness, then waiting for dawn, had been worth it. They seemed to have succeeded in getting away from any slave catcher who might follow them to find Jordan and Micah Parker.

"I can't believe it!" Libby exclaimed. "Jordan and his daddy are safely on their way in the wagon. We can walk down the street without wondering if someone will know that they're fugitives."

Libby took a deep breath, just enjoying the fresh air, still cool with the morning. Thinking about how everything had suddenly turned out all right, she laughed aloud. "Not only are Jordan and his daddy together. We have the stolen money!"

But Caleb was more cautious. "You mean we know where the money is. We don't have it in the right places. The money from Jordan's church isn't safe till he turns it over to John Jones in Chicago. And we still need to get your pa's money to Galena by August fifteenth."

Libby knew exactly what Caleb was saying. Galena was in the northwest corner of Illinois, while they were still near the center of the state. For two weeks they had tried to stay ahead of the clock to find money stolen from Libby's father, who was captain of the steamboat *Christina*. But now Libby felt impatient with Caleb. She didn't want anything to spoil her excitement about all the good things that had happened.

Though only a few inches taller than Libby, Caleb walked faster. Just then he reached for Peter's slate. While still walking, Caleb tried to write. Finally he gave up and stopped long enough to scribble, "I hope we hear from Libby's pa. That would make it much easier to find each other."

Holding up one hand, Peter wiggled his fingers. "See?" Because he could hear until he was seven, Peter knew how to speak. "It'd be easier if you learned to spell with your fingers. You can talk even when you walk."

Caleb grinned, returned the slate, and set out again. With Libby and Peter half running to keep up with Caleb's strides, they hurried the rest of the way to the Springfield train depot.

Libby's thoughts leaped ahead, even more quickly than her feet. "Can you imagine what Pa will think when he hears our story?" she asked Caleb. "I can't wait to give him the stolen money and see him pay off that loan!"

Caleb's blue eyes held a warning. "If we don't find your pa, he won't get to Galena by Saturday. He'll lose the *Christina*!"

Again Libby pushed aside Caleb's words. "That's five days. Pa will make it in time. I know he will. We'll find him. We'll give him the money, and everything will be all right."

"If nothing else goes wrong."

Like a clanging bell, Libby heard the words in her mind. *If nothing else goes wrong.* She remembered the fugitive slave laws and the danger to Jordan and his father. She remembered all that had kept them from finding the money before now.

Then she pushed her anxious thoughts away. Today, after their long struggle, the sun was shining. Jordan and his daddy were safe. Today only good things could happen.

Inside the depot they found a man using a telegraph. As he jiggled a lever, Libby heard short and long clicks and knew he was sending Morse code. To her it seemed a miracle that a message could fly over a line of wire stretched between two cities.

Eleven days before, when Libby, Caleb, Jordan, and Peter left the *Christina* at Alton, Illinois, Libby's father, Captain Norstad, continued down the Mississippi River to St. Louis. Before separating, they had agreed to use the Alton train depot as a place to leave messages. Only yesterday Libby and Caleb had telegraphed Libby's father to tell him they were in Springfield.

As the telegraph operator looked up, Libby asked, "Any message from my pa?"

"Here you are!" The telegraph operator handed Libby a piece of paper. Eagerly she read it:

GLAD FOR GOOD NEWS STOP
MEET IN QUINCY AUGUST 12 STOP

Libby stared at the message, then showed it to Caleb and Peter. "If Pa is glad for our good news, why does he say stop?" she asked Caleb.

"Stop means the end of the sentence," Caleb told her. "It's like a period. Your pa wants us to meet him at Quincy, Illinois, on Wednesday, August twelfth."

"Two days from now." Libby looked forward to seeing her

father. She wrote to Peter. "We can meet Pa in time."

But Caleb's eyes had that uneasy look again. He turned back to the telegraph operator. "The next train to the Junction at North Bloomington. When does it leave?"

After several more questions, Caleb led Libby and Peter away from the telegraph operator. The depot had two waiting rooms. Both were filled with benches and looked much alike. However, one room was set aside for women and children. The other, for men and boys, had spittoons—small brass pots—for the men who chewed tobacco.

Instead of separating into two rooms, Libby and the boys went outside. Under the shelter of an overhanging roof, they sat down on crates ready to be shipped.

"What's wrong, Caleb?" Libby asked while eating breakfast.

Picking up a stick, Caleb started to draw in the dirt. "We're here," he said, making a round hole that he labeled *Springfield*. Making a second hole, Caleb marked it *North Bloomington*, then drew a line from Springfield.

From North Bloomington Caleb drew a longer line to Chicago. Then he marked the Mississippi River, Quincy, and Galena.

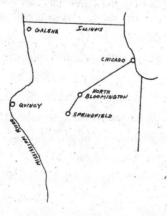

Peter understood. "From the Junction at North Bloomington, Jordan and his daddy will go to Chicago. We'll take whatever trains we need to meet Libby's pa in Quincy. But how will Jordan and his daddy stay safe?"

Safe. As much as Libby wanted to forget the word, she couldn't. *All my life I've wanted to be safe*, she thought.

During the four years after her mother's death, Libby lived with her Auntie Vi in Chicago. Since coming to be with her father on the *Christina*, Libby had learned a new meaning of the word *safe*. She and Pa and Caleb and his grandmother all worked to help runaway slaves be safe. Often Libby longed for a safe place for herself—a place where no danger could touch her or Pa or the people they loved.

Pulling forward a strand of her long auburn hair, Libby started twisting it around her finger. In the early morning sunlight her hair shone red gold. Libby felt proud of her hair and thankful that she had inherited the color from her mother. She also felt glad that she had the same brown eyes as both Pa and Ma. Even now, Libby missed her mother.

Sometimes it was just a fleeting thought—something such as the color of her hair that reminded Libby of days gone by. Other times she felt the deep ache of loneliness. *I wish I could ask Ma what it's like to grow up—to be a girl ready to get married, to be a woman. That would feel safe, too, just talking with Ma.*

Libby's Auntie Vi had worked hard, trying to turn Libby into a perfect lady. It wasn't hard to remember what Auntie said about her. *"Somehow that girl always manages to attract trouble! I just want to give up on her!"*

Those hurtful words had given Libby a bigger wish. "I want

a never-give-up family," she told Pa more than once. "A family that believes in me even when I'm not perfect."

But now Libby felt proud. *Look at all I've done, helping with the Underground Railroad. Someday Auntie will know I'm a person she shouldn't have given up on. I wish she could see me this minute!*

Just then Peter broke into Libby's thoughts. "Let's get the money so we're ready to leave." Without waiting another minute, Peter set out for the police station.

He looks the happiest I've ever seen him, Libby thought. Dexter, the man Peter dreaded, was behind bars here in Springfield.

Little more than twenty-four hours before, in the early hours of Sunday morning, Peter had stood up to Dexter, the thief who stole money from both Pa and Jordan. With courage Peter had revealed who Dexter was—a man who tried to teach him to steal.

But when Peter reached the door of the police station, he suddenly stopped. "I don't want Dexter to see me," he said. "He's really upset with me."

Libby couldn't blame Peter for wanting to stay out of Dexter's way. She dreaded even the thought of what an angry Dexter might do. In spite of the morning sunlight, Libby shivered.

Reaching around Peter, Caleb pulled open the door and walked in boldly. To Libby's great relief she couldn't see the jail cells from where they came in. Libby felt sure the cells were just beyond a closed door. But Peter kept glancing around, as though wondering if Dexter was looking over his shoulder.

"Good morning!" The policeman who arrested Dexter greeted Libby and Peter like old friends. When Libby introduced

Caleb, the policeman stretched out his hand and shook it.

"So you're all together again," he said warmly. "Then I expect you want to travel on."

From a nearby safe, the policeman took the two bags of money he had held for safekeeping. One bag was Jordan's share—the money collected by his church in Galena. The other held the money stolen from Pa's safe on the *Christina*. When the policeman set the two bags on a table, Libby realized they had a problem. "We can't carry money like that."

"I have a basket you can have," he said. "It will look as if you're carrying food for a picnic."

Libby set Pa's bag of money in the basket and covered it with food from her knapsack, then a towel offered by the policeman. Caleb divided Jordan's share of the money three ways. He, Libby, and Peter stuffed the bills in their knapsacks.

As they started to leave, the policeman stopped them. "Just a minute. Your friend Allan Pinkerton left a message for you." Taking an envelope from a drawer, the policeman handed it to Libby.

Libby started to tear the envelope open. She couldn't imagine what the great detective wanted to tell her. Then she noticed how nervous Peter looked. He was glancing over his shoulder again. A line of sweat stood out on his upper lip.

Forgetting the message from Mr. Pinkerton, Libby turned back to the policeman. "How is your prisoner doing?"

"He had one visitor last night—a man I didn't know. Seemed to be from out of town."

By now Peter had edged over to the outside door, and Libby felt sure he wanted to leave. After thanking the policeman for all he had done, she and Caleb followed Peter outside.

When the sunlight caught Peter's hair, he seemed even more blond. But Libby also saw the scared look in his eyes. "What's the matter?" she asked him, using signs Peter had taught her.

As though not wanting to admit how frightened he felt, Peter straightened his shoulders. "When I told Dexter I didn't want to steal, he said, 'If you ever go against me, I'll get even.'"

Dexter had threatened Libby's pa the same way. Holding up a clenched fist, he shook it at Pa, saying, *"If it's the last thing I do, I'll get even with you!"* And Dexter *had* gotten even.

Trying to forget her own memories, Libby wrote on the slate. "You stood up to Dexter anyway. I was proud of you." Yet for that very reason Libby felt afraid.

Peter glanced up from the slate. "Dexter said he'd hunt me to the end of the earth to get even."

Libby couldn't ignore her own scary thoughts. *If Dexter ever got out of jail, what would he do to Peter?*

Again she tried to offer comfort. "Pa says that sometimes we have to pay a price for doing the right thing."

When the scared look in Peter's eyes didn't change, Libby felt sure she had said the wrong thing. Glancing up, she wondered if a cloud had passed over the sun. The morning sky was blue and clear with no clouds in sight. Just the same, Libby's uneasiness would not go away.

By the time they returned to the Springfield depot, a long line of passengers waited to board the train. Caleb hurried into the depot to telegraph Libby's father, telling him to send any message to the train depot at North Bloomington.

As Libby and Peter took their place in line, she noticed a tall, thin man board the railroad car. Libby poked Peter.

"Mr. Lincoln," he said. "Remember how he carried important papers inside his hat? I wonder where he's going?"

Moments after the conductor called his final "All
a-booooard!" Caleb caught up to them. Libby showed her
pass to the conductor, then started up the steps. At the top
she turned for one last look at Springfield. Though she had
been in the city only a short time, she liked it there. She especially loved the big capitol building with its tall pillars and
great dome.

As Peter and Caleb stepped up beside her, the train whistled twice. Railroad cars clanked together, then jerked.

Just then Libby saw a man running down the street. "Stop!"
he cried. "Stop!"

With a *chug, chug, chug*, the train started to roll. Suddenly
Libby saw who the man was. Grabbing Peter's arm, she pointed.
"The policeman!"

As the train picked up speed, the man waved frantically.
"Dexter!" he called. "He escaped!"

"Escaped?" Caleb shouted.

"When I brought him breakfast, he was gone!"

～ CHAPTER 3 ～

Jailbird!

The moving train drowned out the rest of the policeman's words. A few minutes later he was only a tiny dot far down the tracks. In another minute the dot disappeared.

"What did he say?" Peter asked as Libby followed Caleb into the railroad car.

Libby hated to tell him, but Caleb tried. He didn't bother taking out the slate. Instead he finger spelled the letter *D* in the sign Peter had taught them to use for Dexter's name.

"Dexter broke out of jail," Peter said. It wasn't a question. He knew. "When did he escape?"

This time Caleb used the slate. "Sometime during the night. When the policeman brought Dexter breakfast, he was gone."

"So he had already escaped when we were there." It wasn't hard for Peter to figure out the next step. "The policeman ran to the depot, hoping to catch the train before it took off. He wanted to catch Dexter before he left town."

As if forcing himself to be brave, Peter lifted his head. "Dexter might have gotten on this train before we got here. If he did, I'm going to find out right this minute!"

Taking the lead, Peter started through the first railroad car. Libby and Caleb followed close behind. Toward the back of the second car, two seats faced each other. There a group of men huddled together, blocking the aisle for anyone who wanted to walk through. Peter led Libby and Caleb far enough to see what was going on, then stopped.

At the center of the group was a man whose gaze darted from one person to the next. His dark hair was parted almost in the middle and slicked down against his head. His mustache spread wide, curling up at both ends. With long slender fingers he held up one piece of jewelry after another, then spread them out on the seat turned to face him.

Just then a man put down a dollar bill and threw dice across a wooden board. When they rolled to a stop, everyone leaned forward. A cheer went up.

Making sure that all of them could see, the man with the mustache held a piece of jewelry high. When he handed it to the man who rolled the dice, another cheer went up.

Suddenly three men grabbed for the dice. After a brief scuffle, one of them held out his closed fist. Around him, other men threw down money. Gathering it quickly, the man with the mustache made change from a roll of bills.

Libby studied the man collecting the money. In spite of his expensive clothing and his businesslike manner, his face looked hard. As Libby watched, he glanced over his shoulder, as if making sure who was behind him.

Peter waited only a moment longer, then whirled around. Without looking back to see if Libby and Caleb followed, he stalked off. Going from one car to the next, Peter walked as far forward as he could go to get away from the men. There, where two seats faced each other, Peter dropped down.

His eyes flashed with anger. "Did you see him?" he demanded as Libby and Caleb took the seat opposite him. "Did you see Dexter next to the gambler?"

Palms up, Libby shrugged her shoulders to ask, "Where?" She had been so busy watching the man leading the gambling that she hadn't seen Dexter.

"Next to the man who rolled the dice," Peter said. "His back was to us, but I would know him anywhere, even from the back."

So would I, Libby thought. *Brown hair. Blue eyes. Broad shoulders. About five feet ten inches tall. Usually wears a hat, suit, white shirt, and tie. But somehow I missed him.*

Once, Peter had told her that Dexter didn't know how to dress. Though he wore expensive clothes, his suit jacket didn't fit, and his tie often slipped out of place.

"You're sure it was Dexter?" Caleb asked Peter on the slate. When he nodded, Caleb wrote again. "Let's talk to the conductor."

Caleb jumped up and brought the conductor to where they were sitting. "My friend wants to tell you something." Caleb motioned for Peter to go ahead.

Without wasting a moment Peter started in. "You have a man on the train who escaped from jail last night. The Springfield police arrested him early Sunday morning for stealing money from two different people. He's sitting with that bunch of men who are gambling."

The conductor drew back. "How do you know?"

Seeming to read the conductor's lips, Peter answered,

"I helped the policeman arrest him." Peter looked toward Libby. "She helped too."

The conductor peered down over his spectacles. "A young snip like you? And this girl helped, you said?" That seemed to make it even worse.

This time Peter looked puzzled, as though he couldn't guess what the conductor had said.

"Please," Caleb said, offering the slate. "Peter is deaf. Please write what you want to say."

Instead, the conductor stared first at Peter, then at Caleb. "You expect me to believe your story?"

"Yes, we do expect you to believe us," Caleb answered. "Peter is not making up a story. He's telling the truth."

The conductor snorted. "You're just youngsters! How do I know you're not trying to make a fool of me? What happens if I accuse a law-abiding man of something he didn't do?"

"Law-abiding?" This time it was Caleb who scoffed. "The man you want is sitting in the midst of a bunch of gamblers. Those men are playing for high stakes—a dollar a throw. A man can work a long time to earn the money he's taking from them."

"You want to get me in trouble?" The conductor shook his head. "You're not going to trick me into making a fool of myself. Say all you like, but I find it hard to believe that an escaped jailbird is on this train."

"Those men are blocking the aisle." Caleb was angry now. "They aren't even letting the passengers walk through the car. They're a nuisance to the women and children on board. They shouldn't be allowed on this train!"

"And I am the conductor, young man! I am running these

cars and taking care of passengers. Perhaps the three of you are the ones who should be thrown off this train."

The conductor stomped off, then looked back. "Young whippersnappers! I'm not going to fall for a trick like yours!"

When the conductor left them, the railroad car seemed strangely silent. Feeling both scared and discouraged, Libby stared out the window. The train was passing through prairie that stretched for miles around them. Wherever there had been enough water, prairie grass as tall as Libby waved in the wind. Between the long stems grew blue and white flowers with now and then a scattering of red. Even now, in the morning, heat seemed to rise from the ground in waves.

Looking at the flowers, Libby breathed deep and tried to put away her anger at the conductor's refusal to help. Only then did she remember Allan Pinkerton. Besides being an excellent detective hired by railroad companies to protect passengers from crime, Mr. Pinkerton played an active part in the Underground Railroad. Reaching into a pocket of her dress, Libby pulled out his letter. Quickly she read the short note, then showed it to Caleb and Peter:

I need to go on, but if you travel through the Junction I can help you. Before I was a detective I was a cooper—a barrel maker. In the neigboring city of Bloomington, I have a friend named Ryan O'Malley who has the tools I need. I'll stop there and make a barrel big enough for your largest freight. Ryan also has barrels

for smaller freight. If you want
extra barrels for the Christina, ask
my friend for whatever you need.

Caleb's pleased grin lit his blue eyes. "Barrels are just *exactly* what we need! I was wondering how to hide Jordan and his father. Mr. Pinkerton probably knew they needed to pass through the Junction. We're even headed in the right direction!"

A moment later Caleb said, "We just have one more thing we need to figure out. We've got to do something to protect Peter. If Dexter sees him . . ." Pointing to Peter, Caleb gave Dexter's sign name, then their secret sign for *Danger!*

But Peter straightened, sitting tall as if not wanting anyone to fight his battles for him. "I'll make sure Dexter doesn't see me. I've done that before."

Again Caleb gave the sign for Dexter, then pointed to himself. Using a combination of signs and writing, Caleb explained. "I can recognize Dexter, but he doesn't know me."

With Libby it was different. "Dexter knows you," Caleb said. "He knows you stopped him from getting what he wanted."

"Caleb's right, Libby," Peter said. "You stopped Dexter twice—once with Jordan, once with me. He knows you, and he'll never forget your red hair."

Uneasy now, Libby pulled a long strand forward. The light through the window brought out the auburn color. As always, the deep red and gold and the length of her hair filled Libby with pride.

"It's your red hair that's the problem," Caleb said.

Libby's stomach tightened. She didn't like the way this conversation was going. More than once she'd heard Caleb make plans to rescue someone. When Caleb planned something, he meant to see it through, and as far as Libby knew, he always did. Deep inside, Libby had a feeling that she didn't want to know what Caleb was about to say.

Now he pointed at Peter. Then Caleb looked Libby straight in the eyes. When he was sure he had her attention, he began writing on the slate so that Peter would understand. "Something bothers me, Libby. Even if Peter manages to hide, you will give him away."

~ CHAPTER 4 ~

Libby's Red Hair

As she read Caleb's words, Libby's stomach turned over. She knew where this was heading, all right. Now Caleb signed *Dexter*, then wrote on the slate as he talked to Libby. "He'll take one look at you and figure that wherever you are, Peter and Jordan will be close by. He still wants to find both of them."

Swallowing hard, Libby tried to push down the panic she was starting to feel. More than once, what Caleb said had proved to be right. In southeastern Iowa and northeastern Missouri, where Caleb was known as an Underground Railroad conductor, slave catchers always took a second look at him. Then they started hunting for whatever slave he might be helping.

Libby also knew that people noticed her because of the color of her hair. While living in Chicago, Libby had liked that feeling. When she walked down the street, heads turned, giving her the attention she wanted.

My hair is part of who I am, Libby thought. *People like my hair. Seeing it, they like me.*

But now Caleb pointed to Libby's hair. Making the sign for Dexter, he drew his finger across his throat, then pointed to Peter.

As Peter's eyes widened, Libby got the message. Caleb was sure she would put Peter in danger. As much as Libby wanted to believe Caleb was wrong, she knew he was right.

In a small voice she asked, "What should I do, Caleb?"

Caleb started writing. He showed the words to Peter, then said to Libby, "You'd better dress like a boy."

Peter grinned, as though the idea struck him funny, but Libby made a face at Caleb. "I don't want to look like a boy. I like being a girl."

"But for Peter's sake you'll do it," Caleb answered calmly.

Libby stared at him. "This isn't a joke, Caleb."

"I agree."

"Then stop playing with my life. I'm *not* going to dress like a boy."

"I've got an extra shirt you could wear." Caleb bent down to pick up his knapsack. He pulled out a wrinkled-looking shirt.

Libby wouldn't even think about it. "So now I'm supposed to look lumpy and messy and at least ten pounds heavier!" Instead of taking the shirt, Libby moved as far away from Caleb as the seat allowed.

But Peter was also digging in his knapsack. "I've got an extra pair of overalls you could use. You're skinny enough to wear them."

"Peter!" Libby exclaimed. Then she remembered to write on the slate. "You're just as bad as Caleb. I don't want to wear your old overalls. I don't want to look like a boy!" For good measure she underlined *don't* three times.

Paying no attention, Caleb reached into his knapsack again and pulled out a straw hat. Crushed and bent out of shape, it wasn't even clean. Libby hated the look of it.

"You can cut your hair and wear this," Caleb said.

"Cut my hair?" Libby couldn't believe his words. Frantically she reached up with both hands. Grabbing the long strands on either side of her head, she hung on for dear life. "Caleb, you can't be serious!"

When she looked into Caleb's eyes, she knew he was. He only nodded, moving his head up and down three times to make sure neither Peter nor Libby missed what he was saying.

With every passing moment Libby felt more desperate. "What about Peter?" Libby pointed to him and used the sign for *Run away from someone!* Holding out her left hand, she swished her right hand against her left palm with a swift upward motion. "Peter is the one who needs to hide. How will he do it?"

Peter knew exactly what Libby was asking. "I'll watch for Dexter every minute. I've done it before. I can do it again."

Libby shuddered. Looking into Peter's eyes, she guessed more deeply than ever before how difficult Peter's life had been. No wonder he wanted to live with Pa on the *Christina*. No wonder Pa had told Libby, "Watch out for Peter." But the last thing Peter wanted was to have someone treat him like a baby. He had already told Libby so.

Now, strangely, Libby felt proud of Peter—proud of all that he was in spite of Dexter trying to teach him to steal.

But my hair? Libby asked herself, desperate again. *How can anyone, even Caleb, ask me to cut my hair?* Libby felt upset just imagining it.

Trying to think of any other solution but that, Libby looked around. Just then two men entered the railroad car. Peter had his back to the men, but it took only one glance for Libby to recognize Dexter. Frantically she began to write, then realized there wasn't time.

Reaching out, she grabbed the hair on Peter's forehead and pulled down his head. In the next instant she turned to stare out the window. Hardly daring to breathe, she prayed that Dexter wouldn't notice her.

It was Caleb who finally said, "Dexter is gone. You're both safe."

Libby's heart was still pounding. As Peter lifted his head, she met his gaze. Libby could barely stand to look into his eyes.

Before now she had seen Peter upset. Yet even when he was scared, he had managed to stay calm and do what was needed. Now the look in his eyes reminded Libby of a rabbit she had once scared up in a garden. He had taken one panicked look at her, then darted every which way, trying to find cover again.

Her own words coming back to haunt her, Libby remembered what she told Pa when she came to live on the *Christina*. *"I want a never-give-up family,"* she had said. *"A family that believes in one another, that sticks together even when it's hard."* Now Peter was part of her larger family—the people who lived on the *Christina*, choosing to help one another.

"Okay," Libby said aloud. In the short time Peter had lived on the *Christina*, she had started to feel that he was like the younger brother she had always wanted. Holding up her hands, Libby made the sign for brother.

Surprise flashed across Peter's face. First, he pointed to Libby. Then he made two fists, crossed his arms, and drew them to himself as if he were hugging someone.

Libby bit her lip as she realized Peter had signed "love." Speaking aloud, he added a word, "Sister."

Libby's gaze met his. Then she picked up her knapsack, the dreaded shirt, overalls, and hat. When she stepped out into the aisle, she headed for the women's room without looking back.

With swift movements Libby changed her clothes. Caleb's shirt was baggy for her and badly wrinkled besides. Peter's overalls were too short, ending just above Libby's high-top shoes. In the mirror she looked just as strange as she feared.

From her sewing bag, Libby took out her small scissors. As she opened and closed the blades, she felt as though they carried a death sentence. Filled with dread, she dropped the scissors on a small table.

Catching up her hair, Libby twisted it into a long rope, then a knot on top of her head. With one hand she held it in place as she tried to put on Caleb's hat. But the hat could not begin to cover her thick mound of hair.

If I had hairpins . . . but Libby had none along—no way of holding such a mass of hair. Even with pins, if she made one wrong move, her hair would tumble down. Whoever saw her would know she was a girl.

Libby ran her fingers through her hair. *It took forever to grow it this long. But if I look like a boy and enter a building, I have to take off my hat. If I'm a boy with manners, that is.*

Libby sighed. Reaching into her backpack, she found a cloth handkerchief and tore it into strips. Pulling back her hair, she bunched it together and tied it at the back of her neck. Then she began braiding below the tie.

When she finished the one long braid, she tied it at the bottom. For a moment Libby stroked the braid. The end was soft and curled around her fingers. Again she debated with herself.

Have I thought of everything? Is there any other way to hide who I am?

But no ideas popped into her head. Instead, Libby remembered Peter's scared eyes. Though Libby had lived with her aunt, then her father, she had always been sheltered and cared for. She couldn't imagine having the kind of fear that Peter knew.

Meeting the eyes of the girl in the mirror, Libby spoke aloud. "Okay, Peter, this is for you. If it keeps you safe, it'll be worth it."

With her braid pulled to one side, Libby cut above the top tie. When the long braid fell into her hands, she was unable to throw it away. Spreading out her jean cloth skirt, she rolled the braid inside. Then, swallowing the lump in her throat, Libby started snipping.

Her hair was longer at one side than the other, and her scissors were small and not meant for cutting hair. Yet Libby did the best she could, leaving the back of her hair as long as possible.

Once, she stopped to look down at her clothes. *What if another girl or a woman comes in?* Thinking about how embarrassing that would be, Libby hurried, taking as big a handful of hair as her scissors would cut.

When at last she stood back, Libby was horrified to discover how uneven her snipping had been. Next to her face some of her hair stood out, looking short and clumpy. Behind her ears and across the back, her hair was jagged and long. Libby took up the scissors again to straighten it out. Then she decided it was so bad there was nothing she could do.

For the first time Libby felt glad that she could wear Caleb's bent-out-of-shape hat. Carefully she tucked any wisps of red hair under the hat and once again faced herself in the mirror. The straw brim came down far enough in the back, front, and sides to cover every bit of hair.

Well, Libby thought, *if I'm going to look like a boy no one cares about, I might as well go the whole way*. Bending down, she untied each shoe, pulled out the tongue, and retied the laces below it.

When Libby straightened again, her dark brown eyes met the gaze of the girl in the mirror. With all her heart Libby hated the way she looked. She was changed all right. *Would my Chicago friends know me if they saw me?* Then Libby felt glad that they wouldn't.

Tears welled up in the eyes of the girl in the mirror. As though she were seeing another person, Libby realized the tears were her own.

Whirling around, she faced the door, then remembered. *What if someone sees me, a boy, coming out of the women's room?*

~ CHAPTER 5 ~

To Be a Boy

Like a turtle peering from its shell, Libby poked out her head. Glancing one way, then another, she looked around. To her relief she saw no one and slipped into the hall.

When she reached the boys, she set her knapsack on the floor next to the picnic basket. The knapsack was a small canvas bag that belonged to Pa, and it would not give her away.

As Libby sat down, Peter grinned at her. So did Caleb, and it wasn't hard to guess what they were thinking.

Peter looked down at her feet. "You should smear dirt on your shoes," he said. "And on your face."

Libby scowled at him. Caleb seemed to sense that she was fighting against tears. He said, "Your hair will grow back soon."

Afraid that she would choke up if she spoke, Libby shook her head.

"It *will* grow," Caleb insisted. "Faster than you think." Surprising Libby, he added, "Just wait. It'll be worth it. You'll see."

More than any teasing could have done, Caleb's kindness started Libby's tears again. Quickly she bent down, reached into her knapsack, and pulled out a handkerchief. When she started to blow her nose, Caleb stopped her.

"Libby!"

His one word held such a strong warning that her heart leaped with panic. *Dexter? Where is he?*

But Caleb reached out, grabbed her handkerchief, and closed his fist around it.

Puzzled, Libby looked around at the people sitting nearby. *Now what's wrong?* she wondered.

Close to her ear, Caleb spoke softly. "Is that the best you can do?" Slowly he opened his fist so that only Libby could see. In the palm of his hand lay her white lace handkerchief.

Libby gasped, then started to giggle.

"It's *not* funny!" Reaching into his knapsack, Caleb pulled out a big red bandanna and offered it to her.

The wrinkled square of cloth had no doubt been in Caleb's knapsack for eleven days. It took only an instant for Libby to decide she didn't want to touch it. "No thanks," she said quickly.

"It's clean," Caleb insisted.

"So?"

"So if you want to blow your nose, you better have something besides a white lace handkerchief."

It was Peter who came to Libby's rescue. He, too, had a big red handkerchief, but his was neatly folded, and there was no question about whether it was clean. With gratitude Libby took it and tucked it into her pocket.

It's not going to be easy trying to look like a boy. Leaning back, Libby closed her eyes to rest. She didn't want to even think about the whole problem.

Two minutes later she remembered the words of the free black man who led Jordan and Micah Parker to safety in Springfield. *"If you have trouble, look for a signal."* Even now that Underground Railroad conductor was bouncing along the road to the Junction with his hidden cargo.

"Find a safe house," he had said. With all her heart Libby wanted Jordan and his daddy to be safe.

As the train drew near to the Junction, Libby, Caleb, and Peter talked about what to do. None of them wanted to be around Dexter any longer than necessary. But instead of trying to be first off the train, they decided to mingle with others who were leaving.

"The more of us there are, the more noticeable we'll be," Caleb wrote on the slate. "We should split up."

They decided that Libby and Peter would go in the direction away from the depot. When they felt it was safe, they would circle around to meet Caleb on the other side of the station. Hopefully he would have Jordan and Micah Parker with him. Though traveling by wagon, they had a six- or seven-hour head start and might already be hiding in the freight room.

Because none of them knew North Bloomington or its neighboring city of Bloomington, it was hard deciding where to meet. "Let's look for a place two blocks from the depot," Caleb wrote on the slate.

"Then we'll find a safe house?" Libby asked. "An Underground Railroad station?"

"I hope so."

It was unusual to see Caleb unsure about anything, let alone about where to go. Libby felt the same way. For all of them this was a new city, a new area.

"Just don't be late," Caleb warned. "We don't want to leave Jordan and his father standing on a street with Dexter around."

"Maybe he'll stay on the train and go to Chicago," Peter

said, but his eyes told Libby that he had little hope of that.

Before long the train whistled for the Junction, and they began seeing houses. As the *clickety-clack* of the wheels slowed down, Caleb picked up his knapsack. When the train squealed to a stop, he gave a quick goodbye wave.

"If we have to wait for you, we'll find a way to vanish from sight," Libby said.

"I hope so," Caleb answered. "But don't make us wait. Micah Parker is tall enough to be a marked man."

Finding his way between people, Caleb hurried to the exit. Through the window Libby saw him leave the train and head for the depot.

Then Peter stood up. Libby picked up her knapsack and the picnic basket with the money and followed him into the aisle. As they waited behind the other passengers, Peter turned to her. "Don't forget our secret sign for danger," he whispered.

Libby felt grateful for the reminder. "I'll watch for Dexter," she signed back.

When she reached the doorway, Libby glanced quickly at every man on the platform of the depot. Seeing no one who looked like Dexter, she moved forward to the top step and checked the exits from the train. To Libby's relief Dexter was nowhere in sight. But she and Peter had waited too long. It seemed that everyone who wanted to leave the train had already done so.

"C'mon," Libby motioned and started down the steps.

As she stepped down on the platform, Libby remembered her new role. Taking a quick swipe at the dusty side of the train, she rubbed dirt onto her face, then her shoes. When she straightened up, she realized Peter hadn't followed her.

As though not wanting to trust Libby's word, he stood on the top step, looking around for himself. Finally he stepped down. The moment he stood beside her, Libby realized their danger.

The train kept them from crossing the tracks to where Caleb wanted them to go. If she and Peter walked to the front of the engine, it could start to leave at any moment. If they hurried to the end of the train, they had to pass the car in which the men were gambling.

Is Dexter still there? Libby had no way of knowing, but they could not remain where they were.

Her mind leaped from one possibility to another. *Maybe Dexter is busy talking to the other men. We could just walk quietly past that car. That has to be less dangerous than standing here in the open.*

In that moment Libby made up her mind. With her finger across her lips she said, "Shhh!" Pointing to the end of the train, she started walking, and Peter followed. On the wooden platform their footsteps sounded hollow and quick, as though they were running away. *And we are*, Libby thought.

Picking up her feet, she tried to walk quietly. But Peter stomped along, unaware of the noise he was making.

As Libby turned around to shush him, she glanced toward the railroad car they were passing. Just then a man with brown hair and blue eyes moved into the doorway. He was wearing an expensive suit that didn't fit, and his tie was out of place. Libby's heart jumped. *Dexter!*

From where she stood, Libby could see the coldness in his face. The hard look made him seem he had lived a hundred years being angry. *If we could find a policeman—*

In her panic she saw no one to ask. Signing "Danger!" Libby tipped her head toward the steps. As Peter's gaze followed hers, his eyes filled with terror.

Peter whirled around. In the next instant he ran straight into a tall thin man returning to the train.

As Mr. Lincoln jerked back, his tall hat tipped off and dropped to the platform. In the same moment Peter fell at his feet.

Mr. Lincoln laughed. "Whoa there, young fellow! Hold your horses!"

Peter stared up into Mr. Lincoln's face trying to decide what the man had said.

Bending down, Mr. Lincoln reached out to give Peter a hand. "Let me help you."

After a long look into the man's eyes, Peter took his hand. With one quick lifting motion, Mr. Lincoln helped him to his feet. His eyes showing his fear, Peter looked around for Dexter.

"Well now," Mr. Lincoln said to Peter. "Are you hurt?"

Peter stared at him and finally spoke. "I'm sorry, sir."

After another quick glance around, Peter ducked his head. Dropping down on his knees, he gathered up Mr. Lincoln's hat. One by one, Peter picked up the papers that had fallen out, blew off any dust, and placed them back inside the hat. With each movement he kept his back turned to Dexter.

Still on the steps of the train, Dexter glanced their way. As though seeing Peter and Mr. Lincoln for the first time, Dexter stared at them. Then his gaze moved on.

As if struck by cold water, Libby recalled Caleb's words. *"Dexter will take one look at you and figure that Peter will be*

close by." With another shock she remembered she was supposed to look like a boy.

Then Dexter glanced back. As he stared at Libby, she
slipped her small hands into the back pockets of her overalls.
She could do nothing about the pounding of her heart.

CHAPTER 6

Jacob's Ladder

Again Dexter's gaze slid past Libby. With two quick steps he was on the depot platform, moving away from them.

Peter handed Mr. Lincoln his hat and seemed to shrink behind the tall man. Looking into Peter's eyes, Mr. Lincoln thanked him. "Are you sure you aren't hurt?"

"He's fine," Libby said quickly. "He's sorry he bumped into you."

For a moment Libby looked into the deep eyes. *Could I tell Mr. Lincoln what's wrong? He seems like a person who would help.*

Just then the conductor sang out, "All a-boooard!"

Mr. Lincoln tipped his hat. "Sorry. I'm on my way to Chicago. I need to get back on that train." With great long strides he was off.

Breaking into a run, Libby started after him. When Mr. Lincoln reached the conductor, she stopped. *I'd make him miss the train. Someone like that must have important business.*

The instant that Libby turned back, Peter took off. This time he ran lightly across the rest of the platform. There he jumped down on the grass and raced toward the end of the train.

Afraid she would lose him, Libby took off after Peter. Without a backward look he crossed the cinders, then the tracks. Even then he didn't slow down, but Libby kept him in sight.

When the train whistled its departure, Peter ran even faster. As the train chugged out of the station, he crouched down behind a small building at the back of someone's yard. Libby caught up and knelt on the ground beside him.

For a minute neither of them could speak. When Libby caught her breath, she peeked around one side of the building. Now that the train was gone, she had a clear view across the tracks. Dexter stood next to the depot, looking one direction, then another.

Libby ducked back behind the building. "Peter!" she whispered, then remembered to reach for his sleeve. Libby pointed to the station.

Still kneeling, Peter peered around the building. Ducking back again, he muttered, "I don't like the looks of that."

Libby thought that he meant Dexter. When she took another look, she felt an extra jolt of surprise. The man with the wide mustache stood next to Dexter, talking as if they were old friends. The gambler they had seen on the train!

Shrugging her shoulders, Libby raised her hands, palms up, to ask, "Who is he?"

"Probably the person who helped Dexter break out of jail. He has all kinds of friends like that."

"Friends!" Libby dreaded the thought. The more she learned about Dexter, the more she disliked the way he lived. Taking Peter's slate, she wrote, "Friends who steal?"

Peter nodded. "Swindlers, forgers, counterfeiters. You wouldn't like his friends, Libby."

For a time they waited, kneeling there on the ground, peering out now and then from behind the building. At last the two men turned toward the door of the depot. When they went into the building, Libby and Peter stood up.

Walking quickly, they headed away from the depot, as Caleb had told them to do. The moment Libby felt it was safe, she signed Jordan's name.

Peter understood her question. "Dexter and his friend went into the depot," he said. "Jordan and his daddy would be in the freight room. Dexter won't go there."

"How do you know?" Libby signed.

Peter grinned. "He thinks it's beneath him. He wouldn't mix with the freight unless he thought there was a good reason. Then he'd try to send someone else."

"You?" Libby pointed.

"Me." Peter was still walking fast. "Haven't you noticed how Dexter dresses? How he acts? In public he always pretends he's something he isn't—a big, important businessman."

If only . . . Again the thought leaped into Libby's mind. *If only we could find a policeman. If we could take him to the depot while Dexter is still there.*

For a minute Libby rolled the idea around in her mind. *But what could we say?* Caleb and Peter hadn't been able to convince the conductor.

Even so, the idea wouldn't go away. Two blocks later, when it was time to circle around, Libby took Peter's slate. "Let's find the city marshal," she wrote. "Let's tell him Dexter is here."

The moment Peter read her words, fear leaped back into his eyes. Just the same, he nodded.

From a woman walking along the street, Libby asked directions to the police station. When they got there, the marshal was on duty somewhere else in the city.

Leaving the station, Libby and Peter tried to make up for lost time. Half running, half walking, they hurried to meet Caleb. Even from a block away, Libby could see him.

"Something's wrong," she said. Caleb would not be standing in the open if he had anything to hide.

When they reached him, Caleb signed Jordan and Micah's names, then wrote on the slate. "They aren't here yet."

"So what do we do?" Libby asked.

"We wait," Caleb said. And wait they did.

At the Junction, the city also called North Bloomington, someone had planted thousands of trees. On that hot, sticky day Libby looked for trees large enough to offer shade. She and Peter stayed in a park-like area that surrounded a large house on a rise of land. From there they could see across the tracks to where Caleb sat with his back against the wall of the depot. Nearby was the high platform used for loading freight.

As Libby watched, she grew more and more uneasy. To her way of thinking, there were too many men milling around the depot. With no train in sight, why were they there? Could one or more of them be someone hoping to collect a big reward by capturing a runaway slave?

Then as Libby looked far down a dirt road, she saw a cloud of dust growing larger. When the wagon drew closer, she recognized the driver—the Underground Railroad conductor from Springfield.

At first Libby felt excited. Then she felt scared. Glancing toward Peter, she saw that he, too, was watching the driver.

As the free black man drew still closer, he glanced toward

the depot. Instead of coming straight on, he turned his horses at the next corner and disappeared.

"He's worried too," Libby wrote on the slate. "He sees the men near Caleb."

As the afternoon stretched out, the hours grew long and the temperature kept rising. Finally the men seemed to grow tired of hanging around the depot and walked off in different directions. A long time later Libby saw the wagon from Springfield again.

The moment it appeared, Caleb stood up. At the edge of the platform he sat down and let his feet dangle over the edge. This time the Underground Railroad conductor drove up to the depot. There he directed his horses back toward the platform.

When the wagon stopped, the conductor jumped to the ground and walked around to the end. After a quick look around, he bent down. A moment later Jordan and Micah Parker slipped out from their hiding place in the false bottom beneath the bed of the wagon. As if helping the conductor, Micah started lifting boxes from the wagon to the platform.

Again Caleb stood up. When he walked away from the depot, Jordan and Micah followed at a distance. Libby and Peter also followed Caleb at a distance. Two blocks away, out of sight from the train depot, they all drew together.

Ah! thought Libby. *Jordan and his daddy will get the money to Chicago after all!*

But now they faced a new problem. Walking as if they all belonged together, Libby, Caleb, and Peter went first, with Jordan and Micah Parker behind them. They walked as if it didn't matter that the daylight was still strong, as if it was all right for anyone to see them pass down the street.

"Where do we go?" Libby asked Caleb as he led them toward the neighboring city of Bloomington, where there were more houses than in the newer North Bloomington. Soon Caleb left the busy street on which they walked and cut off to the left. As all of them followed, Libby felt confused.

"Caleb," she whispered finally. "What are we looking for?"

"A signal," he answered.

In the five months Libby had known Caleb, he had never given her such a strange answer. Usually strong and fearless, with every move planned out, Caleb always seemed to know where he was going. As an Underground Railroad conductor, Caleb cared deeply about the well-being of every fugitive he helped. He did everything he could to help them pass safely to the next station.

Now Libby had an awful suspicion. "Caleb, do you know where you're going?"

Caleb rolled his eyes as though he didn't have the faintest idea, then shook his head.

"Did you ask at the train depot?"

"There wasn't anyone to ask," Caleb said. "Something strange was going on. Something I didn't understand. But I suspect there were slave catchers around. The free blacks just melted off in different directions. The man in the freight room looked nervous, and I knew he was afraid to talk to me. So I just waited."

Caleb turned to Jordan and his father. "The conductor in Springfield said to look for a signal. What did he mean?"

Jordan grinned. "Could mean most anything. A light. A statue with a rag on the hand."

"Maybe a song," Micah said. "A drawing of the North Star.

A signal with the hands. A safe quilt."

A safe quilt. Always Libby had thought of a quilt as something soft and warm, something to wrap up in when tired or cold. *What makes a quilt safe?*

Not even Caleb seemed to know because he told Jordan and Micah, "Whatever the signal is, you need to find it. I can't."

"Keep walking," Jordan said as if he had suddenly become the leader instead of Caleb.

A block farther on, Jordan left the street. At an opening in a hedge, he passed between houses and disappeared into a backyard.

Remembering Caleb's words on the train, Libby felt uneasy. *"The more of us there are, the more noticeable we'll be." We're too many people.*

The streets were nearly empty now, with people home eating their evening meal. Just the same, Libby couldn't help but wonder how many people watched from their windows. *We've got to get help soon.*

Micah Parker seemed to feel the same way, for he strolled on, outwardly paying no attention to where his son had gone. Yet he clenched and unclenched his fists, as if growing more nervous by the minute.

Five houses later, he suddenly left them and passed along a short street. Soon he returned, only shaking his head and again walking with them.

With every minute that passed, Libby felt more nervous. It was bad enough to think about Dexter finding Peter, yet if that happened, people would believe Peter was innocent. It was another matter if Dexter or a slave catcher found Jordan and Micah. Lawfully they could be taken back to their owners.

"We've lost Jordan," Caleb said softly, signing the letter *J* to Peter.

"I'll go back," Peter said. "If Jordan and I don't catch up with you, come find us."

Walking on with only Caleb and Micah Parker, Libby felt foolish. *Looking*, she thought. *Looking for what? Jordan and his daddy are looking for any kind of signal. I can at least spot a quilt.*

In the morning before making up a bed, a woman aired out whatever quilts had been used. Sometimes she hung a quilt over a clothesline, other times over a bush or railing. But now Libby wondered, *Is it too late in the day? Have all the women of Bloomington aired their quilts and put them back on their beds?* Jordan and his daddy still had at least two hours of daylight and no place to go.

Then Libby came to an even bigger question. When does an ordinary quilt become a signal?

Soon Jordan and Peter caught up to them. But now Jordan looked over his shoulder often. His father seemed even more uneasy. More than once he glanced back, as if not sure whether he should stay with them. Libby could understand why.

In the past it had been difficult enough to hide Jordan because of his height and proud look. Only recently had Caleb and Libby learned they could help protect Jordan by walking as if they belonged together. For Jordan's father, Micah, it was even more dangerous because of his recent escape from slavery. Posters scattered over a wide area described Micah's height and offered a big reward for his capture. At any moment the wrong person could start trouble.

As Libby tried to push away her uneasiness, Jordan spoke

quietly from where he walked. "Pray," he muttered softly, but Libby heard the word.

Pray, she thought. *Lord, I just want Jordan and his daddy to be safe.*

On the next block, they met two rough-looking men walking along the street. When they stared at Jordan and Micah Parker, Libby felt frantic inside.

Soon the men passed on. Yet when Libby turned around to look, she found one of them still staring at Jordan and his daddy.

Again Libby prayed. *Help us, Lord. Help us find a safe place!*

A few minutes later Jordan spoke in a soft voice. "The Lord says, 'Turn here.'"

More than once Jordan had received strong leading from the Lord—a quiet inner sense of what to do when they needed help. Libby and Caleb had learned to respect what Jordan said because of the way his words proved to be true.

For a block they walked along the side street Jordan had chosen. Soon he said, "Turn again," and they followed another street. A block farther on, Libby caught the movement of cloth on one side of a house. Eagerly she hurried forward.

Outside a second-floor window, a railing surrounded a narrow walkway. Hung over the railing was a quilt made with dark red and blue pieces against the cream color of unbleached muslin. A gentle breeze lifted one corner of the quilt.

In that moment Jordan spoke in a low voice. "That's the signal we need!" Moving quickly into the yard, he led them into a clump of closely grown bushes. There he knelt down.

From between the branches Libby could see the quilt even better. The dark red and blue triangles and squares looked like ladders—steps leading upward.

Libby's mind leaped. *Steps leading up to heaven?* From Jordan, Libby had learned that *heaven* could be a code word. For Christian slaves it meant a place where there would be no more bondage. But slaves also used the word to mean escape from slavery in this life.

As though Libby had asked her question aloud, Jordan began to hum. Soft and low he hummed, almost under his breath. Then just as quietly, he began to sing.

> *"We are climbing Jacob's ladder,*
> *We are climbing Jacob's ladder,*
> *We are climbing Jacob's ladder,*
> *Soldiers of the cross."*

Jacob's ladder! Libby thought. *So I did understand!* From her mother's early telling of Bible stories, Libby remembered how Jacob fled from an angry brother. When far away from home, Jacob used a rock as a pillow and lay down to sleep. That night he dreamed of angels going up and down a ladder between earth and heaven.

Then Jordan whispered, "Squint!" and Libby did.

In that moment she saw it. In daylight the dark blue pieces stood out as lines moving diagonally across the quilt, as though from south to north. As Libby looked at the quilt with her eyes nearly closed, the blue pieces seemed to merge into lines. "Railroad tracks!"

"The Underground Railroad!" Jordan whispered back. "Tracks leading to the Promised Land!"

Down on her knees, Libby waited without moving. The

clump of bushes seemed to have been planted especially for people who needed to hide. Libby and the others watched to see if anyone went in or out of the house. At the same time, they watched the street and the surrounding neighborhood.

As the minutes stretched long, Libby grew more and more impatient. Turning to Caleb, she whispered close to his ear. "If someone takes us in, can I stop looking like a boy?"

"I don't know," he whispered back. "Anyone who hides fugitives knows better than to talk. But there's something else—the rules of the Underground Railroad."

The rules, Libby thought. *The unwritten rules. Most people working with the Railroad know only what they need to know.* And Libby understood why—for their own protection.

The more we tell someone, the harder it is for that person if he's questioned. A person who doesn't know something is innocent if a cruel slave catcher questions him.

Just as Libby felt she couldn't wait another minute, Jordan turned to his father. "You be ready to run if I'm wrong?"

"I be ready to run," Micah Parker answered. "But you run too." Jordan's daddy tipped his head toward the barn back of the house. "I be waiting for you there."

～ CHAPTER 7 ～

The Missing Money

 **W**ith a last careful look for anyone who might pass by on the street, Jordan stood up. Quietly he slipped out from between the bushes and across the lawn to the side door.

As he reached the steps, Jordan started humming again, so softly that at first Libby wondered if she was imagining it. But Jordan rapped quickly on the door, then moved close to an open window.

There his humming changed to singing. Low and clear the words came across the short distance.

> *"Every round goes higher, higher,*
> *Every round goes higher, higher—"*

Suddenly the door opened. A tall young woman looked out. Even from where Libby hid, she could see that the woman was beautiful.

The woman's long black hair was pulled up to fall into loose curls at the back of her head. Tucked at one side behind her ear were blue flowers that matched the deep blue of her eyes. "Come in," she invited in a soft voice.

"There be five of us," Jordan answered.

"I know," she said. "I watched you from the upstairs window."

As Libby and the others crossed the lawn, the young woman stepped back enough to be hidden behind the open door. The moment they all stepped inside, she closed the door.

"Welcome," she said, her voice warm with friendliness. "I'm Annika Berg. Were you followed?"

"I don't think so," Caleb answered. "For the moment we seem out of danger."

"Then I'll get you some food. But if anyone comes to the door . . ." Annika led them up the stairs. In a bedroom she showed them a closet behind a closet where they should hide if needed. "We have a better place in the barn," she said. "From there it will be easier for you to leave if necessary. After dark I'll show you."

Libby's spirit leaped, responding to Annika's loveliness. But even more, her smile was warm and welcoming. *Womanly,* Libby thought. *Everything I'm not right now.*

Just looking at Annika, Libby felt the dirt on her own clothes. Cinders from the train had blown in through the open windows. On that hot August day a fine dust had settled over all that she wore. Even worse, Libby disliked how she looked— her jagged cut-off hair, the wrinkled shirt and overalls. The look of a boy when she wanted to be what she was—a girl.

From where he stood beside her, Caleb touched the brim of her hat, and Libby remembered to take it off. For Libby it was also a reminder not to tell Annika more than necessary. As an agent—someone who ran an Underground Railroad station—she had put herself in a dangerous spot.

In spite of Annika's womanly ways, Libby knew by instinct that she was strong. Only a courageous woman would protect runaways from a cruel return to their masters. In turn, Libby wanted to protect Annika.

When they returned to the kitchen, Annika added corncobs to make a quick fire in the cookstove. "Would you like to wash up?" she asked as though not concerned about making the hot kitchen even hotter.

Libby's spirit leaped. *Yes, I'd like to wash up!*

In an entryway next to the kitchen door stood a bench with a pail of water and a basin. Nearby, a towel hung on a roller. When Libby's turn came, Caleb poured fresh water for her. Just seeing the water, Libby could only think about getting clean. Then as she splashed cool water on her cheeks, she remembered, *I better keep some dirt on my face.*

When she finished washing, a glance in the mirror showed Libby that a streak of dirt still darkened her cheek. But now she faced another problem. *It's hard enough to look like a boy. How do I act like one?*

Annika had pushed a kettle onto the hottest part of the stove. While the soup heated, she made sandwiches. Between two pieces of thickly sliced bread she put cheese and meat. As she invited them to sit down at the drop-leaf table, Libby watched the three boys.

When Jordan picked up his spoon, he kept an eye on Caleb, as though his momma had taught him to take a sharp look when he needed to know what to do.

And Peter? He was stuffing bread into his mouth so fast that he barely chewed it. For a time Peter had lived like an orphan. It looked as if he filled up on bread when there was no good cooking around.

Caleb had the best manners. He said *please* and *thank you* and closed his mouth when he chewed. Libby decided that she'd have to figure out her own way to act like a boy.

With hunched shoulders, she leaned over her plate. Holding her sandwich with both hands, she took the largest bites she could manage without choking.

When Annika served the soup, Libby had another problem. Auntie Vi had taught her to dip her spoon into the bowl, then away, before lifting it to her mouth. Libby started doing as she was taught, then stopped. *I look too dainty.*

Again Libby looked around. Peter had picked up his bowl and held it close to his chin while spooning soup into his mouth. Libby did the same, then decided she could go one better. With the spoon close to her lips, she slurped.

Across the table Caleb glanced up. For an instant he stared at Libby as though thinking, *I can't believe this.*

I'm really doing well, Libby decided, filled with satisfaction. *Caleb must be pleased with how I'm acting.*

When Annika finished serving, she sat down to eat with them. Up close, she looked even more beautiful. Annika was also as curious as Libby.

"Why are you traveling together?" Annika asked, looking first at Jordan and Micah, then at Libby, Caleb, and Peter.

"We're friends," Caleb answered.

"Helping one another?"

Caleb nodded.

"You're an Underground Railroad conductor?" she asked.

"At home," Caleb said. "Not here. I don't know this area."

"And you—" Annika turned back to Jordan and Micah Parker. "Are there slave catchers after you?"

"Yes'm," Micah answered with his gaze down in the way he had been taught by his master. "There be a big reward on my head. On Jordan's too."

Then Micah looked up and grinned as though remembering he was free. "Us Parkers are worth something."

"Caleb said there be a man on the train who knows us," Jordan explained. In the time since reaching freedom, Jordan had learned to look at people when he talked. "We don't think the man saw us come to your house. But he knew we was in Springfield. He sure enough must be wondering where we are."

"And the rest of you?" Annika looked from Caleb to Libby to Peter. "Are you in danger?"

"Peter is," Caleb answered for him.

Annika leaned forward. "Peter?" She waited for him to look up from his food. When he didn't, she asked again. "Peter?"

Still Peter didn't answer. Though her bread was good, even Annika seemed to realize it wasn't that good. She looked at Caleb. "Is something wrong?"

"He can't hear you," Caleb said.

Annika nodded. "So that's the reason for the slate." Standing up, she walked around the table. When she reached Peter, she touched his arm lightly, then touched his slate where he had set it on the floor next to his chair. "May I?"

Though Peter couldn't hear her, he understood and nodded. Annika slipped the slate out of the bag and sat down next to Peter. "Are you in danger?" she wrote.

When Peter looked up at her, surprise filled his eyes. He

glanced toward Caleb, as though wondering how much he should say.

Caleb motioned with his hand. "Go ahead."

Quickly Peter told the story of Dexter, his arrest and escape, and also his cruelty.

"And he's looking for you now?" Annika wrote at last.

"I think so," Peter answered. "But he also wants Jordan. And if he knew Jordan's daddy is here—" Peter didn't have to finish.

"The reward money," Annika wrote.

"Yes."

"Not a very nice man, is he?" Annika wrote.

Peter met her gaze. "Are you afraid?" he asked.

When Annika smiled, her soft skin seemed to glow from within. "No," she wrote. "I'm not afraid. Are you?"

As though a weight had fallen off his shoulders, Peter straightened. "Not anymore," he said.

"Good!" wrote Annika.

"Do you like children?" Peter asked.

"Yes, I like children. I'm a schoolteacher."

"Here?"

Annika nodded and wrote quickly. "When I lived in Philadelphia, I answered a newspaper ad for teachers in the West. I lived in Kentucky for a year, and I've taught here for two years."

"This is your house?" Peter asked, as if wanting to know everything about her.

Annika shook her head. "I'm taking care of it for some people who are gone."

And taking care of anyone who comes through on the Underground Railroad, Libby thought.

Standing up, Annika walked over to a small table and began dishing up a large piece of oatmeal cake for each one of them. In her whole life Libby had never tasted anything better. And she remembered to eat it with her fingers, not her fork.

Then Libby realized Annika had forgotten to give them napkins. Reaching into her back pocket, Libby pulled out the red bandanna Peter had loaned her. Bringing it to her lips, she patted her mouth clean.

Looking up, Libby saw Annika watching her and again felt proud. But Caleb rolled his eyes.

Uh-oh, Libby thought. *What did I do now?* Looking around, she saw that no one else seemed to miss having a napkin.

When they finished eating, Caleb asked Annika for a piece of paper and a pen. Going to a nearby desk, she opened it and offered him a place to sit down.

As Caleb dipped the quill into the ink, Libby watched over his shoulder. "What are you doing?" she whispered.

"I'm writing a letter to the editor."

Libby was curious. "About what?"

"The men gambling on the train. And how they treated other passengers, blocking the aisle and all."

"You think the editor will publish it?"

Caleb shrugged. "I don't know. But if I want to be a writer, I'd better write."

Ever since Libby had known Caleb, he had wanted to become a newspaper reporter and editor.

"But what if—" Libby glanced at Jordan and his father, then at Peter. "What if Dexter sees what you've written?"

Caleb seemed to read her face. "Dexter doesn't know me, remember? It'll be all right, I promise you."

Caleb lowered his voice. "By the way, don't be so dainty about the way you wipe your mouth."

When he finished writing, Caleb asked for directions to the newspaper office and the town cooper. Libby felt sure Caleb was planning to check the barrels Allan Pinkerton had promised.

As soon as it was dark, Annika told Jordan and Micah how to find the secret room in her barn. Slipping away one at a time, they moved like shadows across the back lawn. But Annika said nothing to Libby.

Where will I sleep? Libby thought with growing worry. *Can I tell Annika I'm a girl?* With all her heart Libby wanted to stay in the house, safe and close to the teacher.

Soon Peter followed Jordan and his father. By now Caleb had returned. When he started to leave for the barn, Annika stopped him. From the lean-to off the kitchen, she carried a large tub.

Just seeing the tub, Libby felt sick. Annika set it down at one side of the kitchen, close to the pantry door. "Help me with the water, will you?" she asked Caleb.

Between them they carried a huge pail of steaming water from the stove and emptied it in the tub. Then Annika added cold water from two smaller pails. Reaching down, she put her hand in the water to test it. "Just right for such a hot day," she said.

All Libby could think about was how good it would feel to be wet all over. Again she wondered where she would sleep. Then Annika said, "I thought you'd like to sleep in the pantry tonight."

Libby stared at her. "In the pantry?"

"You'll be more comfortable there," Annika answered.

At the side door, Caleb turned back. Libby saw his grin before he disappeared.

"Would you like a bath first?" Annika asked as she opened the door to the small room off the kitchen.

The outside wall of the pantry had a large window to let in light during the day. The other two walls had floor-to-ceiling shelves filled with dishes, large bowls, and containers of food. On a counter along one side were a bowl of eggs, a large coffeepot, and jars filled with root beer.

Annika set a candleholder on the counter, then drew heavy curtains across the windows. She and Libby pulled the tub into the small room.

"When you finish, slide the tub back into the kitchen. We'll empty it in the morning." Again Annika left the room, this time returning with blankets, sheets, and a pillow. "If you lay these on the floor, you'll have a good bed."

Filled with relief, Libby started to thank her. But Annika only said, "If you need me, I'll be in the room right down the hall."

Just taking off the overalls and shirt made Libby feel better. For a long time she lay in the tub, letting the lukewarm water soak into her skin until she finally felt cool. But Libby couldn't help but wonder about Annika giving her a special room and a bath besides. *I don't think I'm fooling her. But if Annika knows I'm a girl, why doesn't she say something?*

When Libby finally stepped out of the water, she couldn't bear to put on the covered-with-cinders boys' clothing. Instead, she rummaged in her knapsack for her own clothes. *By the time Annika sees me in the morning, I'll look like a boy again*, Libby promised herself.

Dressed in a nightgown and white robe, Libby opened the pantry door. Careful not to slosh the water, she dragged the tub into the kitchen, then spread out the blankets to make a bed. After blowing out the candle, she lay down on the pantry floor.

The blankets made a soft mattress, and Libby thought she'd fall asleep at once. Instead, she lay wide-awake, thinking about all that had happened that day: Dexter's escape, riding on the train, running through the streets of Bloomington.

Then Libby's thoughts tumbled further back. Getting the money from the Springfield policeman. Putting it in the picnic basket.

Libby gasped. *The money. Where did I leave Pa's money?*

In the kitchen? No, Libby couldn't remember carrying it inside.

On the train? Libby couldn't think of anything more awful than losing it on the train. *No, I was carrying it when Peter ran into Mr. Lincoln.*

Where then? When Peter and I hid behind that small building?

With each leap in her thoughts, Libby felt more frightened. Desperate now, she forced herself to think. *Where? Where? Where?*

Now she felt angry with herself. *How could I possibly lose so much money? How could I forget about it?*

Then she remembered why. *Because I was concerned about Jordan and his father. I was also thinking about Peter.*

While Libby knew it wasn't an excuse for carelessness, she felt glad. Inside, something had changed that she cared more about people than money. Libby's panic disappeared.

As her thinking cleared, she remembered kneeling in the bushes outside the house. *I set the basket on the ground. That's where I left it!*

Libby jumped up. Without making a sound she opened the pantry door. *If I just creep out and get the basket, I'll be right back in. No one, not even Caleb, will know I did such a stupid thing. But I have to creep out without Annika knowing.*

On tiptoes Libby crossed the kitchen. When Libby turned the large key in the lock, it grated with a loud squeak.

Libby paused, her fear returning. *How well can Annika hear?*

Too well, Libby decided. *Teachers and parents always hear better than anyone else.*

Holding her breath, Libby stood there. Listened. Waited. When Annika did not appear, Libby tugged at the kitchen door. When it quietly opened, Libby stepped out on the porch. Her bare feet moved soundlessly across the wood and down the steps. Racing across the lawn, she slipped between the bushes. The basket was there!

Picking it up, Libby lifted the napkin and checked under the remaining food. In spite of her carelessness, the money was still there.

Relief flowed through Libby. *All I have to do is get back to the pantry without Annika seeing me!*

As Libby wiggled out from the bushes, she heard a noise down the street. With one swift movement Libby crept back into the bushes. She had barely reached cover when the noise became clearer. *Footsteps! Heavy footsteps on the boardwalk. The walk that passes within five feet of where I am!*

Loud and hollow the footsteps sounded. And coming this way. Just listening, Libby knew it had to be men. Cringing, she drew back as far as she could into the bushes.

Then she glanced down. Her white robe caught and held whatever light the night offered. If the men glanced her way, they would spot the white cloth showing between the leaves.

In terror Libby looked around. Earlier that day she had stayed under the bushes. Now she crept close to the white picket fence next to them. Making herself as small as possible, she began to pray. *Keep me safe, Lord. Please—just keep me safe.*

Leaning into the fence, Libby did not move. Between the boards she peered into the next yard and saw two men come into view. One of them walked with a louder step than the other, as if his boots had higher heels.

The hollow sound on the boardwalk filled Libby with terror. Each step hammered away at her heart. *Clump. Clump. Clump.*

~ CHAPTER 8 ~

Mysterious Delivery

Closer and closer the men came. Libby peered into the darkness, trying to see their faces. Instead, she began to hear the sound of their voices.

As the men came even with Libby, they passed not more than five feet from where she hid. In that moment she heard their words. "He must be carrying that money I stole from him. If I see him with a carpetbag, I'll know."

Libby gasped. *Dexter! Dexter talking about Jordan.*

Even worse, Libby knew that if Dexter glanced her way, he might see her, crouched and hiding. Filled with panic, Libby pressed so hard against the fence that her arms began to hurt. *What if Dexter turns to look?*

But Dexter passed on, still talking. "When I collect the reward money, I'll accuse that boy of stealing. I'll say he stole that money from *me*."

As the sound of Dexter's voice faded away, Libby waited. Gradually the hollow clump, the footsteps of the man with Dexter, moved off in the darkness. Even when Libby could no longer hear the thud on the boardwalk, she stayed where she was.

At first she felt so afraid that she could not even think.

With her thoughts tumbling every direction, she became more confused by the moment. *Jordan. Dexter had to be talking about Jordan.* When the members of his church in Galena asked Jordan to carry their gift of money to Chicago, he used a carpetbag—a cloth bag with handles. Today Caleb and Peter carried that money from Springfield for him. But tomorrow—

Tomorrow Jordan needed to travel to Chicago. There he would turn the money over to John Jones or someone else who helped fugitive slaves reach safety in Canada. But if Jordan carried a carpetbag, a knapsack, or anything that could hold something important—

Libby didn't want to even think about what could happen. It would be bad enough for Jordan to be caught by a slave catcher. Jordan would be hauled back and beaten unmercifully by an angry master. But to be a runaway slave caught with what Dexter said was stolen money?

Libby's whole being filled with dread—dread so deep that she pushed it away, knowing she had to figure out what to do.

Without making a sound, she picked up the basket with Pa's money and crawled out from under the bushes. Running lightly across the grass, she headed for the porch, tiptoed across the boards, and pushed open the door.

Inside the kitchen, Libby stood by the door and listened. Here, where there was less light than outside, she waited until her eyes grew used to the darkness. Then she closed the door without a sound.

Moving slowly, she crept across the floor to the table. Trying not to bump into chairs, she felt her way around the table. When she reached the pantry door, she congratulated herself. *I made it!*

Just then she heard a noise down the hall. Stepping inside the pantry, Libby closed the door. Moments later she heard footsteps along the hallway. *Annika. Annika walking in the dark of night.*

Libby lay down on her bed of blankets but held her head off the pillow, listening. From the kitchen came the sound of quiet movements that told Libby Annika was trying not to wake her. But then Libby heard one unmistakable sound. The big key turned, grating in the lock.

She'll know I was outside!

Libby dropped her head to the pillow. As careful as she had been, it had not been enough. Annika would know that she herself had not failed to lock the door.

When at last the teacher passed back down the hall to her room, Libby slipped under the top sheet. But she still could not sleep. *I've got to think of a way that Jordan and his daddy can carry the money safely.* If they were accused of stealing, what would happen to them?

Hours later Libby fell asleep, still not knowing what to do.

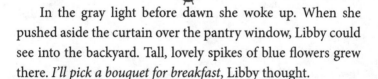

In the gray light before dawn she woke up. When she pushed aside the curtain over the pantry window, Libby could see into the backyard. Tall, lovely spikes of blue flowers grew there. *I'll pick a bouquet for breakfast*, Libby thought.

Then she remembered, *I'm supposed to be a boy. Would a boy pick flowers for breakfast?* Having had no brothers, Libby wasn't sure.

Though she hated the idea of wearing boys' clothing again, Libby changed into the wrinkled shirt and too-short overalls. Feeling grateful there was no mirror in the pantry, Libby pulled a brush through her hair. But when she rolled up her white robe, she found black dirt along the hem, and more dirt on Annika's once clean sheets. Getting down on her knees, Libby tried to brush out the dirt, but dark smudges remained.

Libby sighed. It wasn't easy to live something she wasn't. Though she wanted to protect Peter, Libby didn't like pretending that she was a boy. She just wanted to be herself.

The day dawned bright and warm—so warm that Libby knew the heat would soon be overwhelming. She wished she were on Pa's boat where she could feel the water around her. Better yet, she wished she could go swimming. Long ago Pa had taught her how in case she ever fell off the boat. Since then Libby had become a strong swimmer. But when she lived with Ma's sister, Auntie Vi hadn't approved.

Once Vi had caught Libby swimming in the Chicago River. Just thinking about it now made Libby grin. At first she had wondered if her aunt thought it was dangerous. Soon Libby discovered it was more.

"How could you?" Auntie Vi had stormed. "How could you do anything so unladylike?"

To Libby's relief Caleb was first to come into the kitchen. Sitting at the drop-leaf table, she told him all that had happened in the night. The worst part was her fear for Jordan and his daddy. "What if they're found with what Dexter says is stolen money?"

Immediately Caleb knew what to do. "When they leave here, they'll be in barrels. But they need something that takes less room and isn't as noticeable as a carpetbag. Two money belts would do it. They could divide the money between them so neither one carries so much."

"But where will we get a money belt?" Libby asked.

Then she remembered. Sometimes Pa wore one when he needed to carry a large sum of money to the bank. "How much time do we have?"

"The man with the barrels will come this morning. When he pulls up at the barn, he'll open the doors and drive inside, as if he's making a delivery. Jordan will creep into one of the empty barrels, and his daddy will use the extra large one Allan Pinkerton made for him."

"And the man will drive them to the train?"

Caleb nodded. "To the loading platform. I'll follow at a distance to make sure the barrels are put on the train to Chicago."

"What will happen when they get there?"

"Mr. O'Malley—the cooper—told me that the Underground Railroad has a man working in the Chicago freight room. When he sees a certain label on top, he knows that a fugitive is hiding inside. He gives those barrels extra care and rolls them to the back part of the room. When it's safe, someone will take Jordan and his daddy to where they need to go."

Libby didn't like the idea of Jordan and Micah in something that small. She couldn't help but think how hot it would be inside a barrel, especially when she already felt sticky with heat.

"What if they need to get out?" Libby asked.

"They can push the lids off their barrels from inside."

"But how do they breathe?" Libby asked.

Caleb led her outside. At the corner of the house was a barrel to catch rainwater for washing clothes. Heavy metal rims circled the outside of the barrel, holding the pieces of wood together. Between the two center rims was a good-sized hole plugged with a cork.

"If a barrel holds liquid, its owner puts a spigot in here," Caleb explained.

"And if there's no cork or spigot, it's a breathing hole!" Libby felt relieved. It seemed so simple, and a simple plan often seemed the best of all.

Feeling better about how Jordan and his father would reach Chicago, Libby thought back to the problem of how to carry the money. "I know what to do," she said. "I'll use a bit of Pa's money to buy cloth and rawhide bootlaces. I'll sew each of them a money belt."

Caleb grinned. "And you'll go to the store looking the way you do?"

Libby scowled at him. It wasn't hard to remember how awful she looked. Caleb didn't need to remind her of it. But how could she do what she needed to do without lying?

Then Libby had an answer for Caleb. "Before I go, I'll write a note asking for what I want. I won't say anything about who wrote it. I'll just lay the note on the counter."

As soon as the general store opened, Libby set out. At the counter along one side of the store, she put down the note.

1 yard of light brown, heavy cloth
1 yard of rawhide bootlace

It took only a minute for the clerk to find and cut the right size cloth. "But I'm out of bootlace," he told Libby.

When she paid for the cloth, he gave her change and

directed her on to another store. There Libby paid for what she needed and hurried out.

At Annika's house again, she collected her sewing bag and went upstairs. Finding a table, she laid down the cloth and cut it in half. Spreading out one piece, she folded up the bottom third. Then, using one of Pa's dollars as a guide, she sewed straight lines to make a pocket. Soon she had pockets from the left side to the right.

Taking the top third of the cloth, Libby folded it over the bottom third. Finally, she sewed a length of rawhide on each end of the pockets.

Working quickly, Libby started a second belt. She was just finishing that one when Caleb came in.

When Caleb saw what she had done, he was pleased. "Both Jordan and his daddy are wearing loose shirts. Unless someone searches them, no one will see the money belts. And you're just in time!"

As a wagon rolled into the yard, Caleb took the money he and Libby and Peter had carried and divided it in half. Libby helped him slip the bills into the money belts. Caleb stuffed the belts into his knapsack and raced out of the room.

From an upstairs window, Libby saw the wagon filled with barrels pull up to the barn. When Caleb opened the large double doors, the wagon rolled inside, as though for a delivery.

In that moment Libby heard footsteps. Hollow-sounding footsteps from the boardwalk, but with a lighter thud than the strange clump of the night before.

Only two houses away, Dexter was coming along the boardwalk. Looking from left to right, he was searching for someone.

As she watched from above, Libby's fists tightened with nervousness. "Caleb!" she wanted to cry out. "Close the doors!"

In the next minute he did, but then Libby had a new fear. *What if someone opens the doors when Jordan and Micah are climbing into the barrels? What if Dexter sees them?*

Closer and closer Dexter came. As he reached the wide path leading to the barn, he stopped. In that moment Libby remembered. *I haven't seen Peter this morning. Where is he?*

~ CHAPTER 9 ~

Libby's Shopping Trip

As though someone had tipped him off, Dexter stood in the path, waiting and watching. After a few minutes he started toward the barn. He was halfway there when the large double doors opened.

Caleb? Libby wondered.

But Caleb was nowhere in sight. Instead, the driver walked out, alongside his horses. With one glance at Dexter, he left the doors open, climbed to the high seat, and called, "Giddyup!"

When the horses drew close, Dexter had to step out of the way. Yet he seemed to count each barrel. As the wagon passed into the street, Dexter turned to the barn.

Through the open door, Libby saw stalls for horses off to one side. At the back of the wide space where wagons unloaded hay, two barrels sat on the dirt floor.

Dexter had reached the barn when Annika hurried out of the house to ask, "May I help you with something?"

Dexter stopped in his tracks. "Just wondering about those barrels."

"The barrels," Annika answered. "Oh yes, the barrels." She sounded as if she was stalling for time. Walking over to the barn, she closed one door. "Are you a barrel lover by any chance?"

The question seemed to throw Dexter off balance. For a moment he hesitated, then said, "Yes, I like barrels. Could I see how yours are made?"

Annika laughed. "Oh, you're trying to tease me. You wouldn't really want to see our barrels. They're just extras for the people who live here."

Closing the second door, Annika dropped the wooden latch in place. "It's good to meet you, Mr.—" She paused, waiting.

Instead of giving his name, Dexter lifted his hat. "Good day, miss."

As he turned toward the street, Annika started for the house. Yet she stood on the side steps, waiting, until he was a block away.

I wonder if he's going for a search warrant, Libby thought. *Annika made sure he stayed interested in those barrels.*

When Annika calmly entered the house, Libby turned away from the window. *Peter,* she thought. *I've got to find him this minute.*

To Libby's relief Peter was sitting at the kitchen table. When Libby saw the late breakfast Annika was making, she sat down at the table next to Peter. Seeing how happy he looked, Libby put off telling him about Dexter. Instead, she watched Annika work.

Libby felt curious about her. "Where is your husband?" she asked.

Annika stiffened. "My husband?"

Uh-oh! Libby thought. *I asked the wrong question.*

Then Annika smiled, and the tension between them broke. "I haven't married," she said.

"But you're so pretty," Libby blurted out.

"I'm only twenty-six. Plenty of time to get married yet."

Still, Libby wondered about it. She knew girls who had married long before they were twenty-six.

When Libby didn't answer, Annika laughed. "You're wondering if I'm an old maid."

Libby felt uncomfortable now. That was exactly what she had been thinking.

Annika's eyes turned serious. "I don't want to marry unless I find a man of God—a man who loves and cherishes me the way I want to cherish him."

Libby had never heard someone put it like that before. Sure, Pa was a Christian. And Ma had been one too. But to give that as a reason for getting married?

Annika's breakfast was as mouth-watering as it looked. In spite of all she had eaten the previous evening, Libby heaped her plate with pancakes, eggs, and ham, then took a second helping. She always had a good appetite. Now since she looked like a boy, she felt free to eat like one.

Libby ate till she was stuffed, then gobbled even more. Remembering what Caleb said about using a napkin, Libby thought of a boy in her Chicago classroom. Whenever he drank milk, he had a white mustache. Libby didn't know how to get a mustache without spilling milk down her front. But she could do what he did. Lifting her arm, she wiped her sleeve across her mouth.

No longer able to put it off, Libby knew she had to tell Peter about Dexter. When she touched his hand, Peter looked up.

"What's wrong?" he asked, searching her face.

Libby signed Dexter's name.

A scared look leaped into Peter's eyes. "Here?"

Libby took the slate. "He was outside." Starting with the night before, she wrote quickly, telling Peter about the two men.

Peter stopped her. "You said one was Dexter. Who was the other?"

Libby shrugged her shoulders. She remembered the heavy thuds of the man's footsteps. Standing up, she stomped her way across the floor. But Peter still had a question in his eyes.

Sitting down once more, Libby took Peter's hands and plunked them on the table as if someone were walking. This time Peter seemed to understand.

Picking up the slate, Libby wrote again. "Dexter came back this morning. He looked in the barn."

As Libby wrote, Annika came around behind Libby and watched. Finally Annika asked Libby for the slate.

"You don't need to be afraid, Peter," she wrote. "If Dexter comes back, he won't find you, no matter how hard he searches. You can hide in the secret room I showed you upstairs."

When Peter smiled, the fear left his eyes. "I think I'll just stay around the house today."

"Now," Annika said to Libby, "since Peter can't go outside right now, will you carry in some wood for me?"

As usual, Annika looked right at Libby when she spoke. *She doesn't know my name,* Libby realized. *Come to think of it, no one has mentioned it in front of her.*

When Annika showed her the woodpile, she asked Libby to take from the section of smaller pieces cut for the cookstove. As Annika went back into the house, Libby stared at the wood and wondered what to do. *If I hold the wood close to me, I'll get all dirty.*

With her hands on both sides of the wood, Libby picked up three small, round unsplit logs. Heading for the house, she carried them out in front of her. But when Libby reached the porch, she needed to set down the wood in order to open the door.

Again she picked up the wood. Still carrying it out in front of her, Libby dropped it into the bin near the cookstove. When she looked up, Annika was watching her.

On the third trip Annika stopped her. "Why don't you carry a bigger load? It will save you trips."

This time Libby picked up four pieces. As she carried them between her hands, one piece fell on her foot. "Ow, ow, ow!" she cried out.

As she hopped around on one foot, Annika came outside. Giving Libby no sympathy, she only said, "Let me show you a better way."

Using her right hand, Annika loaded wood onto her left arm. "This is how boys do it."

"The way boys do it?" Libby asked weakly.

Annika smiled. "Don't you think I can tell that you're a girl?" Carrying an armload of wood, Annika started toward the house.

Libby sighed. After cutting off her hair and trying so hard, she had been found out. She could only be glad it wasn't Dexter who had seen through her disguise.

This time Libby stacked wood on her arm the way Annika showed her. She had to admit it was easier, and she could even open the kitchen door. But when Libby entered the kitchen, she asked Annika, "How did you know?"

Laughter filled the teacher's eyes. Picking up a napkin, she daintily patted her lips.

"That's all?" Libby asked. "That's the only way you knew?"

"Well, no," Annika admitted. "You're doing a good job. But the way you talk doesn't fit the way you look. You've had a good education, haven't you?"

Libby nodded. In spite of her best efforts to ignore Auntie Vi's teaching, Libby had turned into more of a lady than she thought. Now she felt foolish about all the ways she had tried to act like a boy. "You didn't say anything."

"I knew you must be doing it for a good reason," Annika answered gently. "I wanted to help you—to protect you."

"You did." Libby thought back to the bath and having her own private room. She had felt protected and cared for. "Thanks."

Annika smiled. "Don't mention it. But if you go outside at night, please lock the door when you come back."

By the time Libby finished carrying wood, she had decided she didn't want to lose the basket again. If she made two more money belts, she and Caleb could divide Pa's money between them.

Still wearing the dirty, wrinkled overalls and shirt, Libby returned to the first store and bought another yard of cloth. Once again she had dirt on her face and the tongues hanging out of her shoes. Again she used her father's money, received bills in change, and used one of those bills to pay at the second store.

Instead of giving her the bootlaces she asked for, the storekeeper glared at her from where he stood behind the counter. "I thought it was you!"

"Me?" asked Libby, startled into speaking. After being found out by Annika, Libby had decided to work harder at not talking.

"Yes, *you*! The good-for-nothing boy who bought laces this morning!"

"Sir," Libby said politely, "what is wrong with buying bootlaces?"

"There is nothing wrong with buying bootlaces! But there's plenty wrong with not paying for them."

Libby felt bewildered. "But I did pay for them!"

The shopkeeper took a long look at her from the dusty shoes to the dirty overalls and shirt, to the bent-out-of-shape hat. Libby felt the hot flush of embarrassment leap into her cheeks.

"Thought you could get by with it, did you?" the shopkeeper asked.

Libby gulped. Had he discovered her disguise? How could she possibly explain she was trying to protect Peter from a crook?

As she tried to think what to say, the man held up the bill she had given him. "This is just exactly like the one you passed off this morning!" Picking up another bill, the shopkeeper waved both of them in her face. "Where did you get these bills?"

"I got them in change at the last store where I shopped!"

"A likely story!" Coming around the counter, the man peered down at Libby. "How could someone like you have so much money that this is your *change*?"

Suddenly Libby felt afraid. She could not possibly tell the shopkeeper that she had carried a picnic basket filled with money all the way from Springfield.

"You gave me counterfeit money this morning!" the shopkeeper exclaimed.

"Counterfeit?" Libby barely breathed. Never in her life had she felt so humiliated.

"Taking goods from a hardworking shopkeeper like me! And giving me worthless money for payment!" The man's face was red with anger. "Well, you won't get by with it!"

As he leaned close, Libby jumped back. Filled with panic, she started to run. But when she reached the door, the shop-keeper was there ahead of her.

Libby tried to pass him, but he grabbed her arm. When she pulled away, he tightened his grip.

"Let go of me!" Angry now, she was frightened too.

The more Libby struggled, the tighter the man held her arm. Dragging her along behind him, he passed through the open door and started down the street. "I'm taking you to the city marshal!"

Libby groaned. *The police? With Pa a million miles away? Who can possibly help me?*

Walking so fast that Libby had to run to keep up, the shop-keeper pulled her along behind him. For two whole blocks the man dragged her along a busy street. With each step Libby took, she saw heads turn.

"See that naughty boy?" one woman asked her son. "That's what happens if you steal!"

Finally Libby discovered it was easier to stop struggling. By now her arm was not only sore. It was bruised. And she was only calling attention to herself.

When they reached the police station, the shopkeeper flung open the door. As Libby followed him inside, she had a quick look at three cells. Rough-looking men filled two of them. The third cell was empty. Just seeing the one chair and cot behind the bars made Libby feel sick.

Her stomach turned over. *I'm going to throw up.* For the first time she felt sorry about the big breakfast she had eaten. *I'm so scared I'm going to throw up all over this place. And if I do . . .*

As she made plans for how she could throw up on the shopkeeper, he jerked to a halt in front of a desk. Looking into the eyes of the city marshal, the shopkeeper drew himself up. As his chest expanded, he finally let go of Libby's arm.

"Marshal Croon, I am bringing you this young thief to stop his life of crime," the shopkeeper said. "This morning he gave me a counterfeit bill. When I realized what it was, he had already left. But I knew I had found the person who is passing counterfeit bills around our law-abiding city."

"That so?" asked the marshal. "And how did you catch him?"

"Just now he came back to my store. Returning to the scene of his crime, he was. He even tried to buy more bootlaces."

"Hmmm." The sharp eyes of the marshal studied Libby. "Stranger in town, aren't you?"

Libby nodded, feeling even more uncomfortable with her dirty, wrinkled shirt and too-short overalls. More than that, she felt afraid. *One look at me, and he thinks I'm a thief.*

Then Libby felt frantic. *What if the marshal discovers I'm wearing a disguise? He will certainly believe I passed counterfeit money!*

"And where do you live, young man?" the marshal asked Libby.

"On a boat." Libby's voice was small.

"A boat?" The shopkeeper snorted. "In the middle of the Illinois prairie you live on a boat?"

"Yes, sir," Libby answered, but her eyes were on the marshal.

"And where are your parents?" he asked kindly.

"Ma died over four years ago," Libby answered. "My pa—I'm not sure where he is right now."

"See?" asked the shopkeeper. "A homeless waif. A good-for-nothing boy. Passing counterfeit money to rob me of my livelihood!"

Marshal Croon leaned forward, looking straight into Libby's eyes. "Is that true, young man?"

Again Libby felt sick. Afraid to open her mouth, she shook her head.

"Speak up!" urged the shopkeeper. "Admit it now. Tell him you're working for a ring of counterfeiters! Tell him—"

"Just a minute!" The marshal held up his hand.

But Libby could think about only one thing. *What if he puts me in a cell with one of those awful-looking men?*

"Is there anyone you know in this city?" the marshal asked kindly.

Annika, Libby thought. Feeling as if she were drowning and someone had thrown her a rope, Libby remembered Annika.

"Yes," Libby answered. But then another thought leaped into her mind. *Annika works with the Underground Railroad. She took Jordan and Micah in. What if I get her in trouble?*

"Yes?" the marshal asked hopefully.

"Yes, I mean, no." Libby stumbled over the words, then wailed, "Oh no, I'm not supposed to lie!"

A puzzled look entered the marshal's eyes. "Why don't you tell me your name?"

"My name." As though every thought had fled her brain, Libby stared at the man. "My name."

"Yes, your name. Can you manage that?"

Suddenly Libby gagged. Frantically she covered her mouth with her hands.

"He's pretending—" the shopkeeper accused.

Turning in his direction, Libby gagged again. This time she was very sick.

~ CHAPTER 10 ~

The Terrible Telegram

When it was over, Marshal Croon spoke to the shopkeeper. "Is there anyone minding your store?"

For the first time at a loss for words, the shopkeeper
shook his head. Turning, he headed for the door.

Standing up, the marshal walked around his desk. A pail of
water stood on a bench near the door.

"You'll feel better if you wash up," the marshal told Libby
as he poured water into a basin.

Libby took her time and spent every moment trying to
think what to do. Like a squirrel running around in a cage, her
mind flew from one thought to the next.

From where she stood, Libby could see the two cells and
the rough-looking men. As fear washed over her, Libby began
to pray. *Jesus, I'm in big trouble. I believe in You, and You better
help me out.*

When she finished splashing water on her face, Libby
saw that the marshal had taken another bucket of water and
cleaned up the floor. Once again he sat behind his desk. This
time he motioned for her to sit down in a chair.

The chair faced him, and Libby felt as if she were sitting
on eggs instead of wood. But then Marshal Croon said, "Now,

I want you to tell me what happened this morning. Without getting all nervous, just tell me the truth."

Libby drew a deep breath. "This morning I went to two stores. At the first store I bought cloth."

"Cloth?"

"To make a money belt."

"So you have a lot of money to carry around."

"Yes." Libby gulped, knowing she had said the wrong thing again. "I mean, no."

The marshal's eyes seemed to cut right through Libby's brain. "You don't look like the kind of person who has a lot of money."

"Oh, but I am," Libby said quickly, again without thinking.

"No wonder the shopkeeper brought you in!" the marshal exclaimed. "For a moment I thought you might be innocent."

"I am," Libby said again. "Really, I *am* innocent."

"Then you'd better start proving it very quickly. I'm having more and more trouble being convinced."

Maybe I better not tell Jesus what to do, Libby thought. *Maybe I should ask Him instead.* This time she prayed, *Jesus, I just want to be safe. Will You help me?*

"Why don't you start by telling me the whole truth right from the beginning?" asked the marshal.

Even Libby knew that would take too long. Instead, she started at Springfield and worked forward from that.

"And are you traveling around the state of Illinois by your-self?" Marshal Croon asked finally.

"I have a friend. If I can find him, that is. His name is Caleb."

With that the marshal sighed. "Why didn't you say so in

the first place?" Looking as relieved as Libby felt, he stood up. "Where might we find this Caleb?"

They tried the newspaper office first, and that's where he was. When Libby walked in, Caleb held up a newspaper. From the excited look on his face, Libby felt sure the editor had published his letter. But then Caleb's glance shifted from Libby to the city marshal and back to Libby again.

Caleb's excitement faded. "What's wrong?" he asked.

Marshal Croon asked Caleb to follow him to the station. When they walked inside, the room still smelled.

As Caleb sniffed, he looked at Libby. "You?" he asked with a grin. "No hiccups, just sick, huh?" More than once Libby had gotten hiccups when she felt nervous.

Embarrassed again, she avoided Caleb's eyes. It was bad enough looking like a boy—a homeless waif at that. It was even worse being dragged through the main street of town to the police station. But to have Caleb tease her besides—

"Have a chair." Marshal Croon broke into Libby's thoughts. "I'll be right back."

The moment the man left, Libby tried to tell Caleb what happened. "The marshal thinks I passed counterfeit money."

"Oh, is that all?" Caleb glanced around and lowered his voice. "I thought something had gone wrong with the Underground Railroad."

"Something *has* gone wrong." She felt even more upset.

"No, I mean something serious."

"You don't think this is serious?" Libby couldn't believe what she was hearing. "After all I've been through—"

But Caleb was already opening the newspaper. "Look!" He spread it out on the desk. "They published my letter to the editor. It's the very first thing I've had in print!"

As Libby read what Caleb wrote, she saw that it was a fine letter. But she was in no mood to tell him so.

"And here—" Caleb pointed to the words printed beneath the letter. "The editor wrote this—"

Libby stared at the words:

Let's thank this fine young person, a visitor to our city named Caleb Whitney, for telling us what happened on the train so we can do something about this disgrace.

In that moment the marshal returned. To Libby's amazement Caleb sorted out all that had happened to them. Quickly he told about the gambling on the train and the men who blocked the aisles so that women and children couldn't get through. By the time Caleb finished, Libby felt sure that the leader of the group was passing counterfeit bills around.

Somehow Caleb even avoided any hint of the Underground Railroad. He made good sense without telling too much. Strangely that made Libby even more angry.

"Do you have any friends here in town?" the marshal asked Caleb.

"Annika Berg," Caleb answered as if he had known Annika all his life instead of two days.

"Annika?" The marshal turned to Libby. "She's one of my good friends." The way the young man spoke her name, Libby felt sure that he liked Annika.

Without wasting another minute the marshal stood up. "Let's go see Annika. If she tells me you're honest, I'll take her word for it."

But Libby was still angry with Caleb. She couldn't believe how he could act so calm in the midst of such difficulty. "Don't you get upset at anything?" she whispered on the way there.

"Only if it's worth it."

Caleb's self-satisfied grin upset Libby even more. "Just once," she hissed. "Just once, Caleb Whitney! I would like to see you get nervous and upset and throw up and—"

When they reached Annika's front door, the young man knocked as if he had been there a thousand times before. As Annika opened the door, a welcome smile lit her face. "Well, hello, Mark!" She didn't seem surprised to see him there. Then Annika's glance took in Libby and Caleb.

"I'm here on business," the city marshal explained as Annika invited them inside. "Are these friends of yours?"

"Why, yes," Annika said quickly.

"You would trust them?"

"With what?" Annika asked, puzzled now.

The marshal's glance took in Libby. "To not pass counterfeit bills knowingly."

"Counterfeit bills!" Annika shook her head. "No, Mark, you don't have to worry about that. If such a thing happened, it was not intentional."

"Good!" The young man smiled, obviously glad that his business was over.

"Would you like a glass of lemonade?" Annika asked, and he followed her into the kitchen.

When Annika had poured lemonade for everyone, the marshal held open the door for her to go out on the side porch. Libby and Caleb took the hint and stayed in the kitchen. But they sat where they could see what was going on.

"Did you notice something?" Libby whispered to Caleb. "Annika never said my name. She never said he or she."

"Did you notice something else?" Caleb asked. "Marshal Croon seemed awfully glad to have a reason to visit Annika."

Through the doorway Libby was watching him. "I think he likes her. I think he wants to marry her."

It made Libby see Annika in a new light. Not just as a courageous, beautiful station agent for the Underground Railroad. Not even as a new friend. But as someone who spoke the truth. *Maybe she really means it when she says she'll only marry a man of God.*

As Marshal Croon started to leave, Caleb told him about Dexter. "He escaped from jail in Springfield, and we've seen him here in town." When Caleb gave a description, the marshal promised to keep a sharp lookout for Dexter.

But after the young man left, Annika told them, "Dexter was here while you were gone. While you were with Mark, Dexter managed to find a man who gave him a search warrant."

"A search warrant?" Libby asked. "Dexter searched both the house and the barn?"

Annika nodded. "He wanted to see everything."

"Did Dexter find Peter?"

"Of course not. Peter hid in our upstairs room."

"He must have been really scared," Libby said.

"I don't think so," Annika said.

"What about the barn?" Caleb asked. "Did Dexter find anything there?"

"Yes, he did." Annika's pleased smile matched the laughter in her eyes. "Dexter found two barrels that had nothing in them but air."

"Where is Peter now?" Libby hadn't seen him since breakfast, and that seemed years ago.

"Out in the barn," Annika said. "He figured out a better way to hide the door to where fugitives stay. He asked if I wanted him to fix it."

"Peter?" Libby asked. "He's only ten years old."

Annika smiled. "Wait till you see what he's doing. He may be ten years old, but he has an inventor's heart."

"Well, it's good we can travel tomorrow," Caleb said. "Jordan and his father are supposed to return on the morning train from Chicago."

"They'll be coming in barrels?" Libby asked.

Caleb nodded.

"And they'll travel that way to the *Christina*?"

Again Caleb nodded.

Just thinking about the *Christina* made Libby lonesome. Strange how quickly the steamboat had become home. But then Libby knew what it was. The *Christina* was where her father was. "I can hardly wait to see Pa again," she said.

"Talking about your father, we need to see if there's a message from him," Caleb answered. "Before we left Springfield, I sent a telegram asking him to send any message here. Want to go with me?"

Libby shook her head. Right now Libby didn't want to even think about facing the world. "I want to stay where it's nice and safe." With all that had happened, she had almost forgotten about Dexter. Now Libby felt grateful for the short overalls and bent-out-of-shape hat she wore when dragged down the main street.

When Caleb left, Libby once again took out her sewing

scissors, needle, and thread. This time she worked on the kitchen table, and Annika helped her.

As they sewed two more money belts, Libby felt glad that Auntie Vi had insisted that she learn how to sew. But Libby still needed bootlaces and felt unwilling to return to the store. When Annika offered some, Libby accepted them gratefully.

With the money belts ready to use, Libby looked forward to traveling on. "If all goes well, I'll see Pa tomorrow night," she said.

"When you travel so much, what does your father do about your schooling?" Annika asked, as if that were the first thing a teacher would want to know.

"Pa teaches us on the boat."

"Oh, he does? What does he teach you?"

"Everything. When we go up and down the river he makes it a geography lesson. When we come into an important port, he expects us to know its history."

Now that Annika asked, Libby realized the importance of what Pa did. "Most of all, he tries to teach us how to live. He wants us to know what it means to believe in the Lord. And he wants us to live what we believe."

Libby thought about it some more. "Pa especially likes to teach the Declaration of Independence. What it meant to our founding fathers. What it means now. We keep coming back to one part—'We hold these truths to be self-evident, that all men are created equal—'"

Annika joined her. "'That they are endowed by their Creator with certain unalienable Rights, that among these are Life, Liberty and the pursuit of Happiness.'"

"You teach the Declaration too!" Libby exclaimed.

Annika smiled. "I teach it often."

When Peter came in, he wanted to show them his new secret entrance in the barn. By putting shelves in just the right place, he had hidden every crack of the opening into the secret room.

"We can use you on the *Christina!*" Libby wrote on the slate, then added four exclamation marks. Peter's pleased smile told Libby how much her praise meant.

In the house again, Annika took them into the sitting room. There she folded back the cover of the large square grand piano. As she started to play, Peter listened.

The thought surprised Libby. Then she realized that was exactly what Peter was doing. He stood leaning against the piano, his hands and ear to the wood. And he truly was listening.

Watching him set Libby to thinking. *So Peter can feel vibrations with a piano. Does it have to be a musical instrument—something like a piano or drum? Or can he feel the vibration of someone pounding on a piece of wood?*

When Annika stopped playing to take a blueberry pie from the oven, Libby asked Peter about it.

"It's just my ears that can't hear," he told her. "There's nothing wrong with my body."

Libby wrote on the slate. "Let's make up some more secret signals."

Judging by Peter's grin, he liked the idea. As Libby went to the piano, he again leaned against it with his hands and ear to the wood.

On the slate Libby wrote *yes*. Without allowing Peter to see, she pounded one key three times.

"Yes," Peter said. Reaching over, he pounded a key three times.

"No," Libby wrote, then pounded a key two times.

When Peter did the same, it became a game. Soon they had figured out secret signals for Libby's name, Peter's, Jordan's, and Caleb's. Best of all, the scared look that had been in Peter's eyes earlier that day was gone.

By the time Caleb returned, Annika had left to talk with a neighbor. The aroma of newly baked blueberry pie filled the air. Libby and Peter sat at the kitchen table, each devouring a big piece.

"News for you, Libby," Caleb said as he dropped a paper on the table.

"Bad news?" Libby's heart jumped. "Did something happen to Pa?"

Caleb shook his head. "No. Nothing like that. But there was another message from him. Something he wants you to know."

Caleb handed her the telegram. Eagerly Libby started to read.

YOUR AUNT VI IS LONESOME FOR YOU STOP

Libby looked up. "Lonesome for me? How can Auntie be lonesome for me?"

"Keep reading," Caleb answered.

FIND VI ON MORNING TRAIN FROM CHICAGO STOP
TAKE HER WITH YOU TO QUINCY STOP
SHE IS COMING FOR VISIT STOP

Libby threw down the telegram. "Auntie Vi is coming for a visit? I can't be reading this. Tell me it isn't true!"

~ CHAPTER 11 ~

The Never-Give-Up Family

When Peter picked up the telegram and read it aloud, Libby discovered it really was true. The words were there in black-and-white, just as awful as Libby had first imagined them. And there was more.

"Your pa said to be kind to your Aunt Vi."

"Kind!" Libby wailed. "That is the last straw! Pa tells me to be kind when she treated me the way she did? She told Pa that I embarrassed her in front of her friends."

"You embarrassed her?" Caleb's blue eyes were as innocent as a baby's. "How did you ever manage to do that?"

"She caught me swimming," Libby wrote for Peter's sake. "She said a proper young lady would *never* swim."

"What's wrong with swimming?" Peter asked. "I'm a good swimmer."

In that time when many people were not able to swim, Libby knew that Peter's accomplishment was important. It was unusual that both she and Caleb were good swimmers. Caleb's grandmother had insisted that he learn when they came to live on the *Christina*. But Jordan did not know how, and it had almost cost him his life.

"I *am* a good swimmer," Peter insisted.

Libby knew that if he said something, it would be true, but she wasn't going to be sidetracked. "It's okay if you swim," she wrote to Peter. "You aren't a girl. Auntie Vi said I'm a tomboy."

"A tomboy?" Caleb asked. "Anyone could just look at you and know better than that."

Caleb looked solemn, but this time Libby caught his teasing. To her it was the final blow. "Auntie Vi said she can't change me into what she wants me to be," she said, forgetting to write for Peter.

"You don't like your aunt?" Peter asked.

"She doesn't like *me*." Then Libby remembered to write on the slate. "She doesn't like the way I act. She wants me to be perfect."

Peter stopped her. "You don't have to write any more. I understand."

Libby stared at him, then pointed to him and nodded, as though saying, "Yes, you would."

Suddenly Libby felt ashamed. *What am I complaining about?* she thought. *When I lived with Auntie for those four horrible years, she just wanted me to be perfect. By comparison, Peter is in mighty big trouble with Dexter.*

Pointing to herself, she wrote, "I'm being silly." Giving a crazy smile, she hoped Peter understood.

He did. Or at least he said he did. "Besides, I'm growing used to how you look."

In that moment Libby remembered her jagged haircut and wrinkled dirty boys' clothing. Filled with despair, Libby ran her fingers through her hair. "I have to face Auntie Vi looking like this?"

"You don't look so bad," Caleb said, as though trying to be

kind. "Your eyes are still the same deep brown color."

"Oh, Caleb, how can you? How can you be so mean?"

Caleb grinned. "And Peter's overalls aren't very short. Only enough to show your scruffy shoes."

Libby could not think of words awful enough to describe how she felt. Instead she said, "Well, I'm not getting on the train looking like this."

"But nothing has changed," Caleb answered calmly.

"Nothing has changed?" Libby spit out the words. "Dexter has been here and gone. Maybe he'll vanish off the face of the earth. I'm going to leave this terrible disguise behind."

"You can't," Caleb said.

"*You* tell me I can't," Libby stormed. "You think you can tell me what to do? You think I'm going to face Auntie Vi looking like this?"

Though Peter had never met Libby's aunt, Caleb knew and remembered her. Just the expression on Caleb's face made Libby angry.

"You can't change," Caleb said again. "We don't know where Dexter is. Peter is still in danger."

Then Libby remembered Peter. A troubled frown in his eyes, he looked from one to another, as though trying to figure out what they were talking about.

"You don't want me along," he said.

"No, no, no!" Libby shook her head, trying to assure him that was not true.

"I cause trouble," Peter answered.

"No!" Again Libby shook her head.

"I will go away," Peter answered. "No more trouble for you. No more fights between you and Caleb."

Now Libby felt ashamed. Grabbing the slate, she tried to explain. "Peter, I look awful. My Aunt Vi won't like how I look."

But Peter headed for the door. "I will leave. I will go by myself. Then you don't have to look this way."

Libby ran after him. "No, no, no!"

His back stiff, his head high and proud, Peter kept walking. He walked right out the door to the barn.

In that moment there was something Libby knew. *I just hurt Peter the way Auntie hurt me.*

For five months Libby had allowed Vi's words to go around and around in her head. For five months Libby had felt that wound deep inside. She didn't want that kind of hurt for anyone, let alone Peter. She was learning to love him like a younger brother.

Pa said that all of us who live together on the Christina *are part of a never-give-up family,* Libby remembered now. *We stick together, even when it's hard. We believe in one another, even if we aren't perfect.*

In that instant Libby made up her mind. Racing after Peter, she grabbed him by the arm and pulled him back to the kitchen and the big drop-leaf table.

"I'm sorry, Peter," Libby signed. Making a fist, she put her right hand over her heart and rubbed a circle as if wanting to wash away all the hurtful things she had said.

The sign was one of the first Peter had taught her. But now he stared down at the floor, refusing to look at Libby.

Libby took the slate. "It's my pride," she wrote. "My pride about how I look. But I will go on the train looking like this."

When he refused to look at the slate, Libby held it under his bowed head. Finally Peter looked up, and Libby saw the question in his eyes. "Why? I am trouble for you."

"No!" Libby wrote. "It's me—my pride about how I look. What if Dexter gets on our train tomorrow? It's more important that you're safe than what Auntie Vi thinks about me."

As though considering her words, Peter sat quietly for a moment. Then he looked her in the eyes and said, "I'm sorry, Libby."

Libby knew he meant more than how she looked dressed in boys' clothing.

"But you and Caleb?" Peter asked as though knowing Libby was still upset. "What were you talking about? What's really wrong, Libby?"

Libby bowed her head, not wanting anyone, not even Peter, to see the hurt in her eyes. Finally she wrote on the slate. "I can still remember every awful word. Auntie Vi said she wanted to give up on me."

Over Peter's shoulder, Caleb read the slate. "Your aunt said she wanted to give up on you?" In that moment Caleb turned serious, as though the whole thing was no longer a joking matter. "I'm sorry, Libby. I shouldn't have made fun of you."

More than any teasing could have done, Caleb's kindness was too much for Libby. Tears welled up in her eyes and ran down her cheeks. That embarrassed Libby even more. Not wanting to cry in front of the boys, she brushed away her tears.

But the pain of words she had thought about for five months would not go away. Instead, Libby started to sob.

Peter patted her hand. Caleb brought out his red bandanna. This time Libby used it, in spite of how it looked from being in his knapsack for twelve days.

When at last she stopped crying, Caleb had made up his

mind. "Annika has already proved that she can be trusted," he said. "When she comes back, let's see if she has any ideas about what to do."

As Annika came in, she looked from one to the other and asked, "What's wrong?"

Caleb started explaining, and Libby added to it. "Pa has never told Auntie Vi about the Underground Railroad, and I can't either."

"If Libby's Aunt Vi let anything slip, Jordan and his daddy could lose their freedom, even their lives," Caleb said.

When they finished talking, Annika told them, "I want to help you. I've finished my job here. The family who owns this house will return in two days."

"Are you sure you want to leave?" Libby asked, thinking about the young marshal.

"It's been an exciting place to live," Annika told them. "Just a few months ago our neighboring city, North Bloomington, was chosen for the teachers' college, the Illinois State Normal University. Jesse Fell—the man who planted twelve thousand trees—worked hard to get the college here. Some say the city will soon be called Normal after the school."

Annika poured herself a cup of coffee. "Last year, right here in Bloomington, the Illinois Republican party was organized. Mr. Abraham Lincoln gave an excellent speech."

"Mr. Lincoln spoke here?" Libby asked. "What did he say?"

Annika grinned. "I don't know."

"But you said—"

"It was such a spellbinding speech that even the reporters forgot to write it down. None of us can remember what he said." A look of mischief filled Annika's eyes. "People are calling it Mr. Lincoln's Lost Speech."

Annika looked from Libby to Peter to Caleb, as though she had already grown to love them the way they loved her. "I'll travel with you to the *Christina*. Then I'll go to Galena or Minnesota Territory. I know a teacher named Harriet Bishop in St. Paul. She'll help me find another teaching position."

"If you went with us, we would be like a family," Libby said.

Annika agreed. "Whenever Caleb needs to transfer Jordan and his father onto another train, you and Peter and I will keep your Aunt Vi busy. She won't notice what's going on."

Annika also understood why Peter was so afraid of Dexter. "When I met him today, I knew he was a man to be feared. Libby, you need to keep your disguise. I'll give you another hat—one that hides your face better."

Twice during the night Libby woke up with the feeling that something really awful had happened. Each time she came fully awake, she remembered that in the morning Aunt Vi would arrive from Chicago. She would think and say her worst.

Why am I so upset? Libby wondered. *I just got dragged to a police station and accused of passing counterfeit money. How can anything be more awful than that?* Yet for some reason facing her aunt seemed even worse.

Then Libby knew what really bothered her. For as long as she could remember she had wanted to please her aunt. For the same length of time, Libby had never managed to do it.

Finally Libby started to pray. *Please, God, I just want to be safe—safe from all the awful things Auntie says and does. Safe from all the terrible things Dexter and his friend might do.*

The next morning Libby was still at the breakfast table

when Caleb said, "I'll walk over to see Mr. Pinkerton's friend again. We'll take the extra barrels for the *Christina* to the depot. Meet you there, okay?"

Today Annika had pulled up her long black hair, but curls escaped around her face. She wore a bright blue traveling dress.

As soon as Annika served Libby and Peter eggs and ham, she started washing dishes. "We need to leave in half an hour," she reminded them while Libby poked at her food.

In spite of how good the breakfast looked, Libby could barely get it down. When she finally stood up and brought her plate to Annika, she found the teacher looking at her.

"What's the matter, Libby?" she asked.

The kindness in Annika's voice went straight to Libby's heart.

"You'd better tell me," Annika said gently. "I think it's something I need to know."

Libby finished her story about Auntie Vi by saying, "She wants me to be perfect—to be a proper young lady. She said I always manage to attract trouble."

Annika's smile had that look of mischief again. "You attract trouble, all right. But you're a young lady, even in boys' clothing."

"I am?" Even the idea of it shocked Libby.

Annika nodded. "You are fast becoming a young lady. It's in you, Libby. That's why it's so hard for you to pretend you're a boy. But for now you must, and because you must, you will."

"For Peter's sake," Libby said quietly.

"For Peter's sake."

In that moment Libby understood Annika better. "Just like you do things that scare you. You hide runaway slaves."

The night before, Annika had brought in the Jacob's ladder quilt. Now it lay over a chair, neatly folded. Annika picked it up.

"Do you remember Jacob's dream about a ladder set on the earth and the top reaching up to heaven? And God stood above the top of the ladder and promised Jacob, 'I am with thee, and will keep thee in all places whither thou goest.' Libby, that's what God is saying to you. 'I am with you. I will keep you in all the places you go.' But if you want God with you, you need to let Him be there."

Annika put down the quilt. "I can't promise that you won't have a bad time today," she said, speaking gently. "I wish I could make that promise, but I can't. You might have a really terrible day. But there's something I want for you—that you find out what God thinks of you."

"What God thinks of me!" Libby nearly laughed out loud. If Annika hadn't been so kind to her, Libby would have scoffed at the idea.

"What God thinks of you," Annika repeated, her voice steady. "That's much more important than what your aunt thinks of you."

Libby wasn't so sure about that. "What can be worse than facing both Auntie and God?"

But Annika only smiled. "Just wait. You'll see."

Putting down the quilt, she hurried off to make sure that Peter was ready to leave. Already the teacher had packed two carpetbags and set them next to the door. Yet a Bible lay open on the table. Now Libby wondered, *What can be so important that Annika leaves her Bible out till the very end?*

Looking closer, Libby saw that the pages were open to

Psalm 16. One of the verses was neatly underlined. It made Libby curious. *A Bible is really valuable. People fill in the pages for family births and deaths. But underline a verse?*

Then Libby read the words, and they seemed to leap off the page. "I have set the Lord always before me: because he is at my right hand, I shall not be moved."

Not be moved? Libby wondered about it. *Does that mean not be shaken? I will not be scared?*

Yes! Libby decided, for now as she thought about the Lord she felt peaceful inside. No longer scared.

Standing there, Libby memorized the verse. *If only I can remember those words. If only I can repeat them to myself, even if something really terrible happens to me.*

~ CHAPTER 12 ~

Auntie Vi's Threat

When Libby was ready to leave, she picked up the signal quilt from where it lay on a chair. For a moment Libby stroked the soft cloth with its neatly sewn pieces. *If it weren't for this quilt, we never would have met Annika.*

When the teacher returned with Peter, Libby offered the quilt to her. But Annika shook her head. "It's yours, Libby."

"Mine?" In a flash Libby remembered the quilts she had given to fugitive slaves for the *Christina*'s most secret hiding place. None of them were as beautiful as this. "Mine? To keep?"

Annika smiled. "In western Kentucky this is called an Underground Railroad quilt. You're part of that Railroad now, Libby. I suspect that sometime you'll need the quilt for a signal. Besides, I want you to have it for a remembrance quilt."

"Remembrance?" Libby wasn't sure what Annika meant.

"To help you remember who you are—a very special girl who is rapidly becoming a woman."

Libby grinned. "Even though I'm dressed like a boy."

Annika smiled back. "Even though you're acting more like a boy all the time."

Together they tucked the Jacob's ladder quilt inside a pillowcase to keep it clean. When Libby stowed it under one arm, they were ready to leave.

Annika had asked a friend to take them to the depot. When they reached it, the train had come in from Chicago. They found Caleb waiting for them. Standing next to the wall at one side of the depot, Caleb spoke quietly to Libby, "He's here."

"He?" Libby caught the worry in Caleb's voice. "Not *they*? Who's *he*?"

Caleb looked around, then signed Jordan's name.

"What happened?" Libby asked.

"The people in Chicago said it was too dangerous for Micah Parker to go back to western Illinois. They wouldn't let him take the risk. He's going straight from Chicago to his family in Galena. Can you imagine the reunion they'll have?"

"Jordan will meet his father there?" Libby asked.

"If all goes well. Jordan should have gone with him, but he knew we wouldn't leave unless he came."

"He's right. We wouldn't have," Libby said. "And if we don't leave, we won't get the money to Pa. And Pa won't make the payment for the *Christina* on time. But—"

"I know." Though Caleb usually managed to hide his feelings, he looked troubled now. "I can't help wondering if Dexter is hiding somewhere, watching us right now. I don't want to even think about it."

Caleb lowered his voice even more. "As soon as our special freight is on the next train, we'll find your aunt."

"We?" Libby asked. "You're going with me to meet her?"

Caleb grinned. "You bet I'm going with you."

"Caleb, that's really nice of you."

"Well, I'm not sure about that. No big hero here." In spite of his concern about Jordan, Caleb sounded like his old self. "If I'm honest, I wouldn't miss your meeting with your aunt for anything."

To reach Quincy, an Illinois city along the Mississippi River, they needed to make a short trip to the next junction north, then change trains two more times.

"I wonder if your pa realizes how hard it is to get to Quincy from here," Caleb said as freight handlers started to unload the barrels from Chicago.

"Well," Libby said, "knowing Pa—"

Caleb finished for her. "There must be some special reason why he wants a longer stop in Quincy. Maybe it has something to do with Avery Turner."

"Avery Turner?" Libby asked.

"Asa Turner's brother."

"Oh yes." Libby's voice was dipped in sugar. "The pastor in Denmark, Iowa." Months ago Caleb had told Libby that she would never live up to what Asa Turner said. He believed that pastors coming to the frontier should marry women who were proud of wearing a jean dress. Now Libby was not only wearing jean cloth. She even wore overalls, instead of a jean cloth skirt.

But Caleb talked on. "Avery Turner lives on a farm north of Quincy. He puts barrels along the river. Runaway slaves swim across and hide in the barrels till it's safe to take the straight road to the Turner farm."

Caleb leaned back against the depot wall, but Libby knew he was seeing everything. When men transferred freight onto another train, Caleb watched every twist and turn of the barrels.

"There!" he said at last. "Our special delivery is all set."

Peter stayed with Annika, as if she could protect him from anything. Caleb followed Libby onto the train from Chicago.

As Libby boarded the passenger car, she had a deep-down secret wish. With all her heart, soul, and being she hoped that Auntie Vi had missed the train. In one swoop that would take care of all Libby's worries.

But as she led the way down the aisle, Libby saw her aunt sitting next to the window at the end of the car. The window was open, and Libby knew that was unusual in itself. No matter how hot it was, her aunt never traveled with the window open. She hated the black cloud that spewed cinders and dust from the engine into the passenger cars.

Having the window open now meant only one thing. Auntie Vi didn't want any ripples in the glass to blur her view of each person boarding the train.

In the middle of the aisle Libby stopped. Feeling as though a cold hand grasped her throat, she knew. *Auntie saw me. She saw me and didn't recognize me.*

Dread so deep that Libby could not move threatened to overwhelm her. A certainty filled her. *This will be even worse than I thought.*

Scared right down to her toes, Libby started to pray. *What is that verse I was going to remember?*

Then Caleb caught up with Libby. When he looked beyond her, Libby knew that he, too, recognized her aunt. But Caleb only said, "Keep going, Libby. I'm right behind you."

When Libby made a face, he warned her, "If you look like that—"

Behind them the aisle was starting to fill up. Libby had no

choice but to move on. As she came alongside her aunt, Libby stopped and cleared her throat.

"Auntie?" Libby asked weakly.

When her Aunt Vi did not turn from the window, Libby spoke again. "Auntie?"

Still Aunt Vi did not turn. From behind Libby, Caleb whispered, "Speak up. She won't bite."

Libby scowled. It was bad enough to have to face her aunt. She didn't want Caleb pushing her too.

Just then Auntie Vi looked away from the window. With a puzzled frown she stared at Libby. "Young man, a passenger train filled with respectable people isn't a place for begging."

Libby gasped. "For begging?"

Filled with the horror of it, she whirled around, ready to run from the car. But Caleb blocked her way.

"Stand up to her," Caleb whispered.

"Stand up to Auntie?" Libby whispered back. Her throat felt dry with even the thought of it.

But Caleb took Libby's elbow and turned her around. As weak as she felt, Libby knew she couldn't get out of this one. If she ran away now, Caleb would never let her live it down.

This time Libby forced herself to use her strongest voice. "Auntie, it's me—Libby."

As though coming from a far country, Aunt Vi focused her gaze on Libby. For a long minute Vi studied her face. Then her gaze traveled down to Libby's dirty, wrinkled shirt, short overalls, and shoes with the tongues pulled out. Finally Aunt Vi's gaze returned to her face again.

"Libby?" she asked, as though not believing her eyes. "Child! What have you done to yourself?"

In that moment Libby remembered every nightmare sentence her aunt had ever spoken. *"I just can't seem to change Libby into what she should be,"* Aunt Vi had told Pa. *"She can't do anything right!"*

Now Aunt Vi lifted the glasses hanging on a chain around her neck. "Just as I thought," she announced. "Not only are you wearing shocking clothes. They are dirty besides!"

"Yes, Auntie—" Libby began.

"Don't 'yes, Auntie' me. I cannot imagine why you came to see me looking like this. Every day during four long years I taught you to be a proper lady. Look what your father has managed to do in five months!"

Angry now, Libby rushed to the aid of her father. "It's not his fault! I'm the one who decided to dress like this. He doesn't know—"

"He doesn't *know*?" Horrified now, Aunt Vi's face flushed with anger. "Do you mean to tell me that my brother-in-law, your father, your poor dead mother's husband, doesn't know you're running around like this?"

"Auntie," Libby blurted out. "I am trying to protect my friend!"

"Protect your friend?"

Libby swallowed hard. *Protect my friend from a man who escaped from jail,* she had planned to say. Just in time she remembered, *Pa will be glad for what I did. But if Auntie has even one hint*—Libby didn't want to think about what would happen.

If Libby could have managed it, she would have disappeared forever. Forever would she run from the wrath of her aunt. Forever would she hide from the words she knew were coming.

"A proper young lady would never look the way you look!"

"Yes, Auntie," Libby answered politely.

Trying to get as far from her aunt as possible, she stepped back.

"Ow!" Caleb exclaimed when Libby landed on his foot. Instantly Caleb clamped his mouth shut, as though not wanting to make things worse.

Suddenly Libby remembered. "Aunt Vi, Pa said I should find you and help you transfer to another train. We're supposed to meet him in Quincy."

With Caleb's help, Libby led her aunt up the aisle. As they boarded the next train, Peter and Annika followed them.

To Libby's relief her aunt chose a seat with other empty seats around it. As her aunt settled herself next to a window, Libby stood in the aisle. By now she remembered that a proper young lady always made introductions. She would begin.

"Auntie, I would like to have you meet my friends."

Standing aside, Libby motioned to Caleb. In the heat of the August day, his blond hair hung down on his forehead. Streaks of sweat lined his face, but as far as Libby was concerned, he had never looked better.

"This is Caleb Whitney," Libby said proudly. "Caleb is a cabin boy on the *Christina*."

But Libby got no further.

"A friend?" Aunt Vi demanded. "A cabin boy is your friend?"

Libby stared at her. She had forgotten that Aunt Vi always insisted on choosing Libby's friends. More often than not, those friends were dull and uninteresting—even stiff-acting with their desire to please Aunt Vi's mysterious sense of who was worthy to be Libby's friend.

Angry now, Libby straightened to her full height. "Yes, Auntie, Caleb is my friend. Caleb is Pa's friend too. Pa says he would trust Caleb with his life."

Libby turned. "Caleb, this is my aunt, Mrs. Alexander Thornton."

"I'm very pleased to meet you," Caleb answered, even more politely than Libby.

Linking her arm with Peter's, Libby drew him forward. Hopefully her aunt would at least be courteous to him.

"This is my friend Peter Christopherson," Libby said. She refused to give even a hint that on their trip down the Mississippi Peter also worked on the boat.

Libby took the slate from Peter's bag. "This is my aunt, Mrs. Thornton," she wrote, though she had no doubt that Peter already knew.

When Peter gave his polite "How do you do?" Aunt Vi nodded back. For the first time in Libby's memory, her aunt seemed to have run out of things to say.

Then Annika stepped forward. With her quick glance, Aunt Vi looked over the young woman from head to toe. Annika stood Aunt Vi's gaze without flinching. Instead, she smiled.

"I'm Annika Berg," she said when Libby's tongue failed her. "I understand you are Libby's aunt."

As Aunt Vi daintily offered her hand, Libby knew that at last here was someone who could please her aunt. Gentle and warm, Annika was every bit the lady that Aunt Vi liked.

An empty seat faced the one Aunt Vi had chosen. Annika gracefully dropped down opposite Libby's aunt. As though facing a coiled serpent, Libby sat down next to Annika. Caleb and Peter took a seat across the aisle.

As the train chugged out of the depot, Libby desperately tried to think what she could say to her aunt.

"Uncle Alex?" Libby asked. "How is he?"

That was enough for Aunt Vi. For the next twenty minutes she filled the air with news of Uncle Alex. His business had taken him to Europe, and Aunt Vi spoke proudly of his many accomplishments. But only one thought filled Libby's mind. *Auntie isn't lonesome for me. It's Uncle Alex she's missing.* Though Libby hadn't wanted to see her aunt, it hurt to believe that she was just filling time until Uncle Alex returned.

The train ride across western Illinois to the river seemed endless. As though trying to protect Libby, Annika stayed next to her when they changed trains again. When they passed through Peoria, Aunt Vi asked Annika about her husband.

"My husband?" Annika asked.

Guessing what might be ahead, Libby dreaded her aunt's answer.

"Surely a young woman your age is married."

"My age?" Again Annika sounded polite, but Libby saw the sparks in her eyes. It was one thing for someone Libby's age to make a mistake in Annika's marital status. It was quite another for Aunt Vi to do so.

"If you are asking, I am twenty-six," Annika said. Without giving Aunt Vi time to answer, Annika stood up and left for the women's room.

"Twenty-six!" Vi sniffed as soon as Annika was out of hearing. "She must have a really terrible attitude if she's that pretty and an old maid."

This time Libby refused to answer. As she stared out the window, words went around and around in her mind, joining the *clickety-clack* of the wheels. *An old maid, an old maid, an old maid.*

The words hurt Libby. Because Annika had chosen not to be married did not make her an old maid. Instead, she was someone very special with a full, interesting life. With her whole heart Libby longed for the endless ride to be over.

Each time they changed trains, Libby, Peter, and Annika kept Aunt Vi busy while Caleb saw to the transfer of Jordan's barrel. At each stop Libby also looked for Dexter and his friend.

At first she felt relieved that she caught no sight of either. Then it worried her. *Dexter knows we need to return to the* Christina. *Has he gone ahead, knowing Jordan and Peter will come there?* With three hundred people on the *Christina* plus freight, it would be an easy matter for Dexter to slip on board and do his worst to Pa.

Near Quincy Annika left them again. As the train crossed fields north of the city, Libby watched from her window. "Oh look!" she exclaimed as they drew close to the edge of a high bluff. From there Libby could see for miles up and down the Mississippi River. The beauty of what she saw lifted her spirits.

Then her aunt asked, "Your father is meeting us here?"

Hot, tired, and miserable, Libby only nodded. Through-out the trip she had watched Aunt Vi, then Annika, then Aunt Vi again. *When I grow up, I know who I want to be like*, Libby thought. *It's not hard to figure out.*

Aunt Vi looked down at Libby's overalls one more time. "I'm warning you. I'm not going to let your father get by with having you act like this!"

Libby's stomach flipped over. She had no doubt where this was headed. Twisting the cloth of Peter's overalls between her fingers, she stared at her hands without speaking.

But her aunt talked on. "If you're ever going to turn out right, you need to live with a woman of quality like me."

After learning how good it was to live with Pa, Libby couldn't imagine anything worse. Deep inside, Libby felt like crying. As the tears started to blur her sight, she pushed them down. She was too proud to show anyone, let alone her aunt, how much she hurt.

When Libby finally looked up, she realized that Annika was standing in the aisle, listening. Knowing that the teacher had heard Aunt Vi embarrassed Libby even more. As if her life depended on it, she stared out the window.

As Annika sat down next to Libby, the engine slowed to a crawl to pass down a steep grade. Directly ahead, the Mississippi River stretched a mile wide. Coming into the thriving city of Quincy, the train passed between a limestone bluff and the river. Libby could only feel glad that the trip was finally over.

With a squeal of brakes and clanking of cars, the train came to a stop next to a wooden platform. As Caleb and Peter headed for the door, Aunt Vi gathered up her belongings and started after them. But Annika stayed in the seat next to Libby.

When Libby started to stand up, Annika stopped her. "Just a minute. I want to talk with you."

Feeling relieved, Libby sank back down. More than anything in the world, she wanted to put distance between herself and her aunt. But Annika had more in mind.

"There was something I wanted for you today," she said quietly. "In case you aren't able to sense how much God loves you, I want to tell you."

Filled with surprise, Libby blinked back the tears that had been just beneath the surface all day. *God loves* me?

Then her pride took hold. "God loves *everyone*," Libby answered like a child repeating what she had been told. "He loves us so much that He sent His Son to die for us." Yet even as Libby spoke the words, they didn't seem real.

"That's true," Annika said. "God *does* love everyone. God *did* send His Son to die so that we can ask forgiveness for our sins. But do you understand that Jesus died for *you*?"

"Yes." Libby's voice was small. That spring Caleb had told her the same thing and she believed it. But now when Libby tried to think about God's love, her mind edged away from the idea as though she were afraid to test it out. *Does He really love* me?

Annika seemed to have heard her thoughts. "Libby, God loves you as a person. As an individual. Just the way you are."

Out of that dreadful day with her aunt, Libby found that hard to believe. God seemed very far away from her. "How can God possibly love me when my own aunt—a person I lived with for four years—never approves of the way I am?"

"Libby, look at me." The teacher waited until Libby's gaze met hers. "No matter what someone else thinks about you, you are a person God loves. If you forgive your aunt, you'll be able to sense God's love. He delights in you."

"Delights in me?" Libby's laugh was hard, bitter even to her own ears.

But Annika only smiled. "Just wait, Libby. You'll see."

Libby sighed. "I don't think so. I know that God loves everyone. But Auntie wants me in Chicago again. With Uncle Alex gone, she wants someone to fill up her big quiet mansion."

Annika shook her head. "Libby, listen to what I'm trying to tell you."

Instead, Libby looked away. She felt desperate now. *God delights in* me? If Annika weren't such a special person, Libby would have flung the words back in her face. *What am I going to do about Auntie? I don't want to live with her!*

Then like the sun rising over the horizon, Libby thought of the best idea in the whole world. *Pa married Ma while they were still young. Annika is twenty-six. Pa is thirty-four. A perfect match!*

Libby straightened up. *If Pa married again, Aunt Vi couldn't threaten me. She couldn't tell Pa that I have to go back to Chicago.*

∼ CHAPTER 13 ∼
Quincy Fugitive

Meeting Annika's gaze, Libby smiled—the smile she had practiced on the boys in Chicago. Without fail it had worked whenever she wanted to get her own way. "Annika, I should tell you about my pa," Libby began. "He's really nice—a good Christian man."

When a flash of interest entered Annika's eyes, Libby hurried on. "He's very handsome. Tall, black hair, with just a bit of gray right here." Libby touched her fingers to the part of her hair in front of her ears. "Just enough gray to look distinguished. He's not really old."

Libby's words tumbled out as she made sure Pa sounded attractive. "And he runs a good ship. Why, the woman who marries him—"

A grim schoolteacher's look crossed Annika's face. "Just what are you trying to tell me?"

But Libby paid no attention. "I know the perfect solution," she said. "Aunt Vi says I need a woman's influence. That I need to live with her again. But I could stay on the *Christina* if you married Pa."

"My young friend," Annika said in a voice that not even Libby could ignore. "My really young friend—"

Annika's eyes sparked with anger. As her soft white skin flushed red, Libby finally understood. Annika was not only angry. She was offended.

"I came west for two reasons. The Lord led me here, and I wanted to see the country." Annika's voice had a sound Libby had not heard before. "I did not come west to see if I could find a husband!"

As Annika stood up and started toward the exit, Libby had no choice but to follow. She had only one thought. *I made everything even worse!*

When Libby and Annika stepped down from the train, Caleb and Peter stood near Pa on the long platform. Pa was talking with Aunt Vi, but glancing around, as if searching for Libby. With his black hair and captain's uniform, Pa looked tall and distinguished.

Libby's heart leaped. Not until she saw Pa did she realize how lonesome she had been. For a moment his gaze rested on Libby, as if making sure it was her. Then he raised his arm in a wave and broke away, leaving Aunt Vi behind.

As Pa hurried across the platform, Libby raced toward him. When his arms closed around her, he lifted Libby off her feet. His hug was so tight she could barely breathe.

Then Libby giggled, and Pa set her down. His voice was husky as he said, "I'm glad you're home, Libby."

Libby looked up into his eyes and saw that they were wet with tears. He, too, had felt lonely, Libby was sure.

"My dear Libby," he said. "It seems like a year since I saw you last."

Filled with the knowledge of her aunt's threat, Libby said, "Pa, don't ever let me go."

Right there on the platform Pa hugged her again. "Of course I won't let you go. Even when you're so grown up that you leave home, you'll always be right here." Pa touched his heart.

For a moment he searched her face, as though knowing something difficult had happened. "Don't forget," he reminded in a quiet voice. "We're a never-give-up family."

Libby desperately wanted to believe him, but she couldn't forget her aunt's terrible words. *What if Auntie Vi somehow gets her way?* Libby couldn't think of anything more dreadful. She glanced beyond Pa to where her aunt had begun counting pieces in her huge pile of baggage.

Then Pa held Libby off at arm's length. "Judging by the way you look, you must have a story to tell."

"Pretty awful, huh?" Libby asked.

"Pretty wonderful," Pa answered. "You'll be my girl again when your hair grows out."

Pa cocked his head for a better look and grinned. "In fact, you're my girl now, with or without your beautiful long hair."

In that moment Libby remembered Annika. Linking her arm with the teacher's, Libby drew her forward. "Annika, I'd like you to meet my pa, Captain Nathaniel Norstad. Pa, this is Annika Berg. Annika let us stay with her."

"Thank you for taking in Libby and the others," Pa said.

"She put out a quilt," Libby told him.

"A signal quilt?" Pa asked, his voice too quiet for those around them to hear.

Libby nodded. "And she gave the quilt to me." Libby held the rolled-up quilt proudly, like the treasured possession that it was. Not only was it a signal Libby could use if necessary. It also said something more—that Annika believed in her.

As Pa stretched out his hand to shake Annika's, a light leaped into his eyes. Instead of taking his hand, Annika caught up her long skirt and curtsied low. But when her gaze met Pa's, Annika's eyes had the look of mischief Libby was beginning to recognize.

Though there was no depot, they stood on a platform at the end of the railroad line. Beyond the flat land next to the river was the high bluff on which most of the town of Quincy was built.

Pa's boat was tied up near shore with its gangplank down for taking on freight and passengers. As Libby turned toward the river, she had her first good look at the *Christina*.

The side-wheeler was tall and white with her railings gleaming in the last rays of sunlight. On the housing, the arched wooden box that surrounded the paddle wheel, the name *Christina* was printed in large bold letters.

Named Christina *for my ma*, Libby thought as she often did. The four-deck high steamboat was a proud reminder of the mother Libby still loved with all her heart. As Caleb and Peter joined her, Libby gazed at the *Christina. I'm coming home!*

Catching Peter's eye, Libby grinned and thought she knew how he felt. Caleb straightened, standing taller as if he, too, shared Libby's pride.

Even Annika seemed impressed. "You didn't tell me it would be so lovely," she said to Libby.

Seeing the waves lap at the *Christina's* hull, Libby's heart leaped. As though let out of school for the summer, she broke into a run. Caleb and Peter joined her in a race that ended at the water.

When Libby reached the gangplank, she glanced back. Aunt Vi walked between Pa and Annika. Holding her long skirts above the dirt of the riverfront, Aunt Vi looked stiff and stern. She was not pleased by Libby's headlong run toward the boat.

Then from the main deck Libby heard a deep joyous bark. In the next instant Samson tore down the gangplank and headed straight for Libby. As she opened her arms, the big Newfoundland leaped up, nearly knocking her over. Staggering backward, Libby almost fell.

Except for white patches on his chest and toes, Samson was completely black. Down on her knees, Libby threw her arms around the dog's neck. The moment she leaned back, he licked her face. Libby was so glad to see him that for once she didn't mind. "You don't need fancy clothes to recognize me, do you?"

Then she remembered Annika. Standing up, Libby solemnly introduced the dog to her. Annika just as solemnly stretched out her hand. When, in turn, Samson stretched out his paw, Annika laughed. "I'm pleased to meet you, Samson."

Annika then turned to Libby. "This must be your dog—yours alone."

Libby giggled. "It's not too hard to tell."

Now Peter was down on his knees. He, too, threw his arms around Samson as if they had not seen each other for years. When Libby and Peter started up the gangplank, Samson tagged along behind. As Pa, Annika, and Aunt Vi walked onto the main deck, Libby caught the look on her aunt's face.

"Remember the day we said goodbye?" Libby asked quickly. "Pa bought Samson right after you took the train to

Chicago. Pa gave me Samson for my protection."

"Protection!" Vi exclaimed. "It seems to me you need protection from the dog!"

"That's what I thought too," Libby answered. "At first, that is. I didn't want any kind of dog, but now I like having Samson around. He's a Newfoundland, a breed of dogs that rescue people who fall overboard."

Libby rested her hand on the dog's neck. Moving close, he stood as if guarding her. But Aunt Vi sniffed her disapproval.

In the *Christina's* office, Pa saw to it that Annika was given the best available room on the boiler deck. This deck for first-class passengers was above the large boilers that heated water and created steam to run the boat. To Libby's relief, Aunt Vi was given a room at the opposite end of the boat.

When the two women left to get settled, Libby waited behind. "Big present for you, Pa." Proudly she turned over the money belt she had worn. "Caleb will give you the other half."

As Pa took the money his eyes were solemn. "I never thought I'd see this again," he said as he locked the money in the safe. "I can't thank you enough. But I'm even more thankful to God for bringing all of you back safely."

Libby grinned. "Sometime we'll tell you the whole story. Best of all, we made it back on time. You've got three whole days to get from here in Quincy up the river to Galena."

With Samson following close behind, Libby raced up to her room in the texas, the boxlike structure named after the state recently added to the Union. When Libby first came to live on the *Christina,* she thought her room was the smallest on earth. About seven or eight feet wide and six feet long, it had doors on two sides. Now the room was home.

Taking Annika's signal quilt from the pillowcase in which it was wrapped, Libby spread it out on her bed. As she smoothed the cloth, her fingers traced the dark blue pieces that formed a ladder to heaven but also a trail of escape.

Jacob's ladder, Libby thought, loving the story of the fleeing man who received a special dream from the Lord. *The Underground Railroad. Safety.* It felt good just seeing the quilt in her room. It felt even better being back on the *Christina*.

For a moment Libby thought of changing into a dress. Then her curiosity about Pa's plans for Quincy won out.

With Samson trailing behind, Libby went to see Annika. It had taken only a moment for her to set down her two carpetbags. As the teacher made herself at home, Libby felt surprised. She herself had brought a trunkful of clothes when moving from Chicago. But Libby knew without asking that everything Annika had brought along was in those two cloth bags.

There was something else about Annika that Libby thought of only now. *I'm sure that Annika heard what Auntie told me. She also saw what Auntie was doing. But Annika didn't say a word about it. She just tried to help me.*

Leaving Annika, Libby went out on the deck. Here at the end of the railroad line, roustabouts, or rousers, were loading freight brought across land. Sitting down on the wide steps overlooking the forward deck, Libby watched all that was going on. Flopping down beside her, Samson wiggled close for Libby to scratch behind his ears.

A man stood on shore, watching the loading of barrels and crates. He called out, "Careful, careful!" to a rouser who treated the barrels roughly.

Once, Libby would have taken the barrels for granted.

Now because of Mr. Pinkerton's offer of barrels, she watched each one of them. From somewhere in her memory, Libby recalled that Quincy was a big barrel manufacturing city with a number of coopers. Had Pa and Caleb gotten their heads together, working out a new way to safely transport fugitives? Or were these the barrels specially built by Allan Pinkerton?

On the deck below Libby, Caleb stayed close to the gangplank, as though he, too, was just watching. It took only one man to roll some of the large barrels up on the deck. Libby felt sure those were empty ones. Or perhaps they held something that wouldn't be hurt if rolled. It was the barrels that were carried up the gangplank that interested Libby the most.

When two strong rousters picked up a barrel marked *Fragile*, Libby leaned forward. Fragile because of glass or expensive china? Or fragile because a human being hid inside?

When she saw the care with which the men set down the barrel, Libby felt sure it held Jordan. Since runaway slaves usually escaped across the Mississippi River to Quincy, then traveled northeast to Chicago, it seemed unlikely that anyone but Jordan would come the opposite direction, west to the river.

Caleb waited until more barrels were set down next to the one Libby thought might hold Jordan. Then, strolling over, Caleb tipped a barrel just enough to turn it slightly. Libby could only guess why. Was he making sure the breathing hole was open, not set too close to another barrel?

As the crew brought in the *Christina's* lines, Libby forgot about the barrels. To her surprise the steamboat headed south. It made Libby curious. *Why is Pa going downstream, back down the river, when he's in a hurry to get to Galena?*

When Caleb sat down next to Libby she asked him about it.

"It's shallow where we're going," he said. "Boats usually tie up where the train comes in. But your pa has a lot of German immigrants on board. As a special favor, he'll let them off close to Calf Town."

As though Pa's decision was the most natural choice in the world, Caleb pointed to the bluff at least one hundred feet above the river. "German settlers pasture their cows there."

Caleb's years as a conductor in the Underground Railroad had taught him to hide his feelings, especially in times of danger. Yet Libby was starting to know him well enough to sense something deeper. Caleb's quiet, covered-over excitement warned her. Growing more curious by the moment, Libby began looking for anything out of the ordinary.

By now it was dark, and Libby suspected Pa had planned it that way. When the *Christina* tied up, deckhands lit huge torches—iron baskets filled with pine knots and hung out over the bow. From there the cinders dropped safely into the water. As the gangplank went down, German immigrants gathered up all their possessions. With family members carrying a trunk between them, they headed down the gangplank.

When they reached the riverbank, many of the immigrants knelt down on the shore, giving thanks to God for their safe journey. Relatives and friends joined the new arrivals, greeting them warmly. Soon a trail of people wound their way up the limestone bluff.

Still on the wide front steps of the *Christina*, Libby tucked herself close to the wall. There in the shadow Libby could see all that was going on without being seen. Directly in front of where the steamboat had tied up was a large sawmill.

By the light of the torches, Libby looked into a mostly

open shed with a sign, *J. K. Van Doorn and Co.*, on it. The large
rotating saw was now still. Nearby were great piles of logs that
had floated down the river from lumber camps in Minnesota
Territory and the state of Wisconsin.

Other piles held sawn wood—lengths of lumber, or donnage, that steamboats took on board in case they needed to
make repairs. Still other piles held wood to fuel the great furnaces of the steamboats that passed by.

Leaning forward, Libby studied the sawmill. From here Mr.
Van Doorn would be able to see any fugitive who swam across
the river from Missouri. But here, too, in what was called the
free state of Illinois, there were differences of opinion: people
who were against slavery and people who would return slaves
to their owners in order to collect the reward money.

If fugitives come—and Libby felt sure they did—*where do
they hide?*

The open shed with the roof over the large saw looked innocent enough. So innocent that people would not suspect Mr.
Van Doorn of sheltering runaway slaves. Already Libby had
learned that many towns had hiding places in the wood piled
high for steamboats. But here, where the traffic of fugitives was
no doubt heavy, would the woodpiles be enough? And would
they be safe?

Just then Libby remembered Caleb's words about Avery
Turner, the farmer who lived five miles north of Quincy. *"He
puts barrels along the river. Runaway slaves swim across and
hide in the barrels till it's safe to take the straight road to the
Turner farm."*

Now that Libby knew what to look for, the hiding places
were easy to spot. Barrels of all sizes—some big enough to

shelter even the largest man—were pushed without any order along the outer posts of the shed. Some barrels stood upright with pieces of wood sticking out of them. Other barrels lay on their side in just the right position for a tired fugitive to crawl in and go to sleep. With lids lying about, they offered shelter from rain and cold and most important of all, from curious, hate-filled eyes.

Waiting places, Libby thought. *Until Mr. Van Doorn takes fugitives to the next station. Or until a helpful steamboat captain such as Pa comes along?*

Now rousters walked up and down the *Christina's* gang-plank. Leaving with empty hands, they returned with full arms. But soon Libby saw men she did not recognize carrying lumber. Other men carried wood to the furnaces and did not return.

Runaway slaves! Libby knew the men would hide in the furnace room for as long as it was safe. *Will Pa use the extra barrels to help them on their way? If fugitives climbed into the largest barrels, Pa could let them off at a port with a direct railroad line to Chicago. Or Pa could bring them up the river to St. Paul.*

Then, just as Libby decided that everyone who wanted to be on board was hidden away, a shadow next to the sawmill moved. Moments later a young Negro woman stood up. The loose cloth of her sack dress could not disguise that she would soon be having a baby. Yet she ran to the shelter of a great mound of logs.

There the fugitive looked around, then moved on. From woodpile to woodpile she moved, drawing ever closer to the *Christina.* In an open stretch of ground the torchlight caught her face and the frightened look in her dark brown eyes.

Libby strained to see. *She's too big to fit into a barrel.*

Then the woman reached the pile of wood closest to the gangplank. Keeping the logs between her and anyone who might watch, she ducked down. Moments later she peered over the top, looking around, then disappeared again.

As the minutes grew long, Libby guessed what was wrong. In spite of the woman's need to find shelter, she was afraid to walk up to the boat. Afraid she would be caught here on the banks of the Mississippi, after finally reaching Illinois soil.

Libby's heart leaped out to her. *She needs to know if it's safe.*

Safe. Only a short time before, Libby had felt safe when Pa's arms went around her.

Suddenly Libby knew what to do.

∼ CHAPTER 14 ∼

Secret Freight

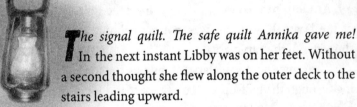

The signal quilt. The safe quilt Annika gave me! In the next instant Libby was on her feet. Without a second thought she flew along the outer deck to the stairs leading upward.

With Samson bounding behind her, Libby raced up the steps. When she reached her room, she snatched the signal quilt from the bed and hurried out to the hurricane deck. As she stood at the highest railing on the *Christina*, Libby remembered that anyone who watched from shore could see what she was doing.

Dexter! Libby thought. *What if he's somewhere about?*

Then she pushed the thought away. Wanting to catch the woman's attention, Libby opened the quilt as though airing it. Once, twice, three times she snapped it in the breeze, then hung it over the railing.

Libby didn't have long to wait. The fugitive behind the logs stood up for a better look. Then the torchlight caught her face, and she dropped out of sight.

Afraid that there wasn't enough light for the woman to see the Underground Railroad pattern, Libby lifted the quilt again, shook it, and draped it over the railing. In the light of the moon the white pieces of cloth stood out against the dark red and blue. Straight as railroad tracks, the white trail led across the quilt.

When the young woman slipped out of hiding and started for the boat, Libby flew down the steps to the main deck. By the time the fugitive started up the gangplank, Libby waited at the top. With one motion of her hand, Libby welcomed her on board.

As Libby headed for the door behind the stairs at the front of the boat, the woman was not far behind. Together they slipped into the cargo area.

The large room was dark, lit only by the torchlight showing through the half-open door. Once that door closed, Libby would have to lead the woman in total darkness.

Then she remembered. Just inside the cargo area that stretched from the front to the back of the *Christina* was a baggage room. There Caleb kept a lantern.

In the sliver of light, Libby fumbled for matches and lit the lantern. "Shut the door!" she whispered. Holding out the lantern, Libby led the woman deeper into the cargo area.

The large open room was filled with freight. Boxes and barrels were stacked high, making weird shapes in the light of the lantern. Soon they passed the entrance to the secret hiding place in the hull of the boat. Instead of stopping there, Libby led the woman to a tucked away spot with more room.

Two-thirds of the way into the cargo area, Libby slipped through an opening between tall piles of freight. Inside was a hidden space, a small room without a ceiling.

As she set the lantern on the floor, Libby had her first good look at the woman. Close up, Libby saw that the loose-fitting dress had been torn in several places. Many of the tears were L-shaped, as though a branch or something sharp had caught at the cloth. All but the most recent-looking tears were neatly mended.

From between two crates Libby pulled out quilts. "For you," Libby said as she spread them out on the floor. "You're safe now. We are your friends."

Gratefully the woman sank down on the quilts. But she sat strangely upon them, holding her feet off to one side.

Libby knelt down on the floor next to her. "I'm Libby," she whispered. "What's your name?"

"I be Sadie." The woman kept her head down, but her gaze darted here and there, as though looking for a way to escape if needed.

Libby saw the fear in Sadie's eyes. "Are there others with you?"

"I come alone. My husband got caught when he was trying to escape." Sadie carried only one thing—a square of cloth knotted into a small bag that she still clutched.

Libby didn't want to even think how frightful it would be traveling by herself in all kinds of weather through woods, swamps, and creeks.

"Bloodhounds was the worst," Sadie added. "And snakes."

"I'll bring food and water," Libby said quickly, knowing that Sadie must have existed on roots and berries.

"Please, Miss Libby. Do you have strips of cloth so I don't hurt your nice quilts?"

Libby moved the lantern closer. Only then did she understand why Sadie held her feet at such a strange angle. In places the skin had grown tough like shoe leather from years of walking barefoot. But in other places—

Libby flinched at the sight of cracks that looked as if they had often been reopened. In some places the blood had dried. In others the blood still ran from deep cuts.

"From one full moon to the next I lived in a swamp before goin' on," Sadie said. "The skin grew soft from walkin' in water and mud and cracked when I walked on them again."

"And you're expecting a baby." Libby felt weak with the thought of it. "What if the baby had been born when you had no place to hide?"

Sadie's smile was like the rising of the sun. "I told myself I couldn't have the baby yet. The Lord promised me this child was goin' to be born in freedom."

Leaning back on her heels, Libby smiled. "Then you can tell this child it's time to be born. My Pa is captain here. He's used to helping babies be born."

From Caleb's grandmother, the head pastry cook on the *Christina*, Libby got food and fresh milk for Sadie. When Libby returned to the hiding place, she found the young fugitive sleeping. Libby set down the food and left, knowing that Sadie would find it when she woke.

When Libby made a second trip with water for washing Sadie's feet, the young woman was still sleeping. But Gran promised to keep a close eye on her.

Quickly Libby searched out Caleb, for he took care of runaways who came on board. If questioned by slave catchers, Pa could honestly say he didn't know about fugitives. But this time Caleb said, "Be sure to tell your pa about the baby."

As Libby started toward Annika's room, she saw deckhands bring in the lines. Putting out from shore, the *Christina* headed north, up the Mississippi River. Libby raced up the stairs and rescued her quilt from the railing. As she spread it out on her bed once more, she felt excited about the way it had helped Sadie.

Libby found Annika on the boiler deck, where first-class passengers took their exercise. The teacher took one look and knew Libby had something to tell her.

"Let's go to my room," she said.

Because of the danger of fire, passengers were not allowed to use candles or lanterns in their rooms. In order to see, Annika left open the door that let in light from the large main cabin. She was just as excited as Libby that the signal quilt had helped the young woman find safety.

"You said that Sadie is about to have a baby?" Annika asked with concern.

"Pa will help her if she needs it," Libby said confidently. "That's part of his job."

Annika smiled. "I had no idea how much was expected of a riverboat captain."

Before Libby could ask the teacher what she thought of Pa, Annika tipped her head for a better look at Libby. "Now that you're on your father's boat again, is there any reason why you need to keep on looking like a boy?"

"I've been wondering about that," Libby answered. "We didn't see Dexter anywhere along the way. He could have left town right after he searched your house and barn."

That bothered Libby. It had been so hard to cut her long hair. She couldn't help but wonder if it had been worth it. "Maybe Dexter headed for the river to watch for Pa's boat. If he did, my disguise didn't make a bit of difference."

"Dexter always knew how to find your father," Annika

said. "When he searched the house and barn, he didn't seem to know you were there. That was protection for both Peter and Jordan, don't you think? But I wonder who tipped Dexter off. Whoever he is, he's a danger to everyone in the Railroad."

Libby didn't know either. She could only remember the men who passed them on the street as they tried to find a signal for an Underground Railroad station.

Again Libby thought about the way she looked. "I just wish I could glue my hair back on."

"Glue it on?" Annika looked startled. "You saved your hair?"

"I braided it before I cut it off."

Annika was delighted. "Then get your braid, and let's see what we can do!"

When Libby returned with her carefully wrapped braid, Annika ran her fingers through the back of Libby's hair. "You left it just the right length!"

From one of her carpetbags, Annika took out what she needed. Fingers flying, she wove the cut-off braid into the jagged hair at the back of Libby's head. To make sure it all stayed together, Annika used hair clasps in four places.

"If you're careful with these barrettes, I think you'll be okay," she said finally. "But don't give your braid a hard jerk. It will fall off."

Using Annika's hand mirror, Libby looked at herself every which way. When she turned to thank the teacher, she tried to speak but couldn't.

"I know you're thankful," Annika said. Her gentle kindness warmed Libby's heart.

In her own room Libby gladly shed the wrinkled boys'

clothing for a dress. It felt wonderful to put on one of her pretty dresses again. She decided to celebrate by returning to the stairway that overlooked the forward deck. Peter was already waiting there, and Samson flopped down next to them. As though half asleep, Caleb leaned back against a crate near the bottom of the stairway.

An hour later all was quiet on the main deck. Moving without sound, Caleb stood up and crept between the deck passengers who lay sleeping wherever they found room. As though knowing exactly where to go, Caleb headed for the large barrel Libby had wondered about earlier.

Sitting down on a nearby crate, Caleb waited. Now and then he glanced around, and Libby guessed he was watching for every possible danger. Finally he stretched out his hand and rapped three times on the top of the large barrel.

I was right! Libby thought as Jordan pushed up the cover.

His head still partly hidden, Jordan looked this way and that. As though his legs felt cramped and stiff, he stood up slowly. After another careful look around, he climbed out of the barrel.

As silent as shadows, Caleb and Jordan found their way back between the passengers. When they reached Libby and Peter on the stairway, all of them crept along the boiler deck, then up the stairs to the hurricane deck.

From there it was only two steps to the narrow deck area that surrounded the texas, the boxlike structure in which Captain Norstad, Libby, and many crew members had their rooms. Pa's cabin was at the front of the boat, just ahead of Libby's room. Caleb motioned them to go farther, where moonlight fell along one side. Sitting down, they leaned back against the wall.

Jordan's face shone with excitement. "Me and Daddy got the money to John Jones!"

As Jordan told about his trip, Caleb wrote quickly for Peter. Tipping the slate toward the moonlight, Caleb used the shortcut words they had figured out between them.

But Caleb soon had to put the slate away. It was too hard for Peter to see, and they couldn't use a candle or lantern.

Libby knew who John Jones was—a free Negro tailor in Chicago who used his business success and big house to shelter runaway slaves. Mr. Jones and his wife had taken in countless fugitives.

"He'll use the money to help fugitives get to Canada?" Libby asked.

Jordan grinned. "Mr. Jones took us to see the roomful of people waitin' to leave. Mr. Jones introduced Daddy and me. He told them about the money from my church. And he said, 'Jordan brought this money for *you*! This money buys your ticket to the Promised Land!'"

Jordan paused. "I never thought—" As though unable to keep on, he broke off.

When he spoke again, his voice was strangely quiet. "When the people in my church chose me to take the money to Chicago, I never knew how hard it would be. And I never thought how *good* it would feel to give the money. All those people in Chicago rose up from wherever they were sittin'. They rose up and clapped for the good people of my church. Then they raised their hands and clapped for the Lord!" Lifting his hands above his head, Jordan showed them.

"When they were done clapping their thank offering, Mr. Jones led them to the boat for the Promised Land. That boat took them all the way across Lake Michigan to Canada!"

Jordan grinned as though still not able to believe it. He wore his proud look now—the look Libby noticed the first time she saw him.

"Do you know what else happened?" Jordan asked. "I met Mr. Frederick Douglass."

"You met Mr. Douglass?" Caleb's voice was filled with awe.

Libby knew what an important person Frederick Douglass was. A former slave, he had spoken openly against slavery in the United States. He had also become a highly respected, much-loved speaker in England.

Jordan held up his right hand, turned it this way and that in the moonlight. "Mr. Douglass shook this hand!"

Jordan stared at it. Then his eyes grew serious. "Remember how my momma named me after the Jordan River? I was just a little boy when she said, 'You is goin' to take our people across the river. You is goin' to lead our people to the Promised Land.'"

Jordan stopped, swallowed hard, then went on. "When my daddy was sold away from us, the Lord gave me a big dream. That we would be a family again, a family living free. If Daddy and I get to Galena—if our whole family be there—we are goin' to know what freedom is!" As though unable to believe it himself, Jordan shook his head.

Jordan met Caleb's gaze. "When you and Libby started teachin' me to read and write, I thought about those people who said I couldn't do it. I just wanted to prove I could. But now it's something more."

Once again Jordan looked at his hand. "When Mr. Douglass spoke, I saw the power of words. Good words help people. Good words change lives."

Jordan leaned forward, talking fast now. "I am goin' to reach high, to get myself educated. I am goin' to learn to speak like Mr. Douglass. And when I do—" Jordan paused as if afraid to say what he was thinking, as if his dream was too big for telling.

"When you do, you will still lead your people," Libby said softly. "You'll lead them in a different way."

When Jordan grinned, Libby knew she had guessed what he was thinking.

"A big dream is worth having," she said. "Someday Caleb and Peter and I will come hear you speak. We'll see you standing up in front of a big audience."

Jordan laughed. "Libby, you sure enough can tease." But Libby knew he was pleased.

Then Jordan grew serious again, as if hearing Mr. Douglass still meant so much to him that he could barely explain. "Just when I see one dream comin' true, the Lord gives me a new one. I thought, 'If I am goin' to be a speaker, what am I supposed to say?' Then I knew. I am goin' to tell people about the Lord!"

In the moonlight Jordan's eyes shone strong and steady. For a time they sat quietly, the sound broken only by the slap of paddle wheels against water. Then Libby remembered that Jordan had to be warned.

"Jordan," she said. "You know how slave owners come north to Minnesota Territory in summer? How they want to go where it's cooler? Some of those people might be on board. And there might be men who read the wanted posters for you."

"What you trying to say, Libby?" Jordan asked. There seemed to be no doubt in his mind that slave catchers would want the big reward on his head. But in the end it was Caleb who told Jordan about Dexter escaping from the Springfield jail.

"Where is Dexter now?" Jordan asked.

"We don't know," Libby answered. "He searched the house and barn where Annika stayed. He was very interested in the two empty barrels."

Jordan grinned. "That man is mighty close on my trail, isn't he?"

"We watched for him all the way here," Caleb said. "With all the changes of trains we didn't catch a glimpse of him. But he's always known how to find Libby's pa."

Jordan guessed the rest of it. "So Dexter could have beat us here. He could have slipped on board and hid himself away from Captain Norstad. If he did, he's waiting to pounce."

"With three hundred people on the boat it wouldn't be hard to hide," Caleb said. "Dexter might have another man with him." Caleb described the man who sold chances on the train from Springfield and probably helped Dexter escape from jail.

"We has to outsmart them." Jordan looked sideways at Libby, then corrected himself. "I mean we *have* to outsmart them." In no time at all, Jordan would sound just as fine as the great speaker Frederick Douglass.

"Libby," Peter asked when they started to go their different ways. "Could Samson sleep in my room tonight?"

Libby stared at him. Peter knew that Pa bought Samson for her protection, that the dog always slept outside her door. But all through Jordan's story and their talk about Dexter, Peter had sat in silence, unable to read the slate in the darkness.

Now Libby remembered that Peter understood Dexter's evil thoughts better than any of them. Why else would Peter want that huge dog inside the small room that he and Caleb shared?

Sick at heart, Libby looked into Peter's eyes. Jordan and Peter would be the first ones Dexter looked for. He had threatened Peter with one thing. *"I'll get even with you if I have to follow you to the end of the earth!"*

Libby felt glad she could loan the dog. Leaning down, she put her hand on Samson's neck and gave him a push toward Peter. "Take Samson with you. He'll like that."

She spoke without thinking, but Peter understood.

You'll like it too, Libby thought when she saw his relief.

~ CHAPTER 15 ~

Footsteps in the Night

Sometime in the dark hours of the night, Libby woke to footsteps outside her room. In those first half-asleep moments she thought it strange. Many of the people with rooms on the texas worked for the *Christina*. At night they walked quietly, trying not to waken the others.

Then, as if jerked out of sleep, Libby was fully awake. The footsteps came from the hurricane deck, just a few feet below the narrow walkway surrounding the texas. Whoever walked there was going around and around, from the bow of the *Christina* to the stern, then to the bow again. Each time the person circled the deck, they passed Libby's small room twice.

Now she heard the rhythm. He walked with a heavy thud, as if his boots had higher heels than most. The footsteps moved away, then returned to pass close again. *Clump. Clump. Clump.*

At first Libby's fear started as a tiny wondering. *Can it be?*

Then as she listened more, Libby knew. The footsteps were the same as those she heard outside Annika's house. *Dexter's friend the gambler! Is he also the man who helped Dexter escape from jail? And is he a forger too? Someone who printed counterfeit money, then used others to pass it on?*

Trying to keep her thoughts from the footsteps, Libby worked it out in her mind. What other explanation could there be for all the counterfeit money in Bloomington? Yes, the man could have gambled to make change, to get counterfeit bills into circulation. But did he also have his own people who spread the money around?

No longer could Libby push her frightened feelings away. With a door on either side of her small room, she felt surrounded. Held by fear, she listened. *Clump. Clump. Clump.*

Filled with panic, Libby grabbed Annika's safe quilt and wrapped it around her. In spite of the warm night, she pulled it over her head.

Safe. The word echoed in Libby's thoughts, reminding her of the runaway slave hiding in the cargo area. *I told Sadie she'd be safe. I thought that here on Pa's boat, I'd be safe.*

Instead, the footsteps filled her with terror. Whoever the man was, he and Dexter worked together. Of that one thing Libby was sure.

I asked You to keep me safe, God. I thought You'd hear my prayer, that You'd protect me. I thought You'd keep scary things away from me.

As the footsteps circled around the back end of the texas and started her way again, Libby pulled the quilt aside to listen. Closer. Closer. Closer the footsteps came. Then they stopped right outside her door.

For what seemed an eternity Libby listened. *Oh, Pa!* she wanted to cry out. She could think of only one thing—wanting to be with her father.

Just one wall separated Libby's room from her father's cabin, but there was no door between. Libby felt afraid to step out on the deck and race to his cabin. The footsteps held her prisoner.

Libby hardly dared breathe. Here, as close as one room away, she could not call out for her earthly father. But her heavenly Father—

In the silence, hearing no movement at all, Libby remembered her prayers. *Lord, I asked You to keep me safe. Safe from what Auntie says and does. Safe from Dexter and his friend. I thought You'd keep me safe from anything bad happening to me.*

Stiff with fear, Libby clutched the quilt around her. *Jesus, where are You? Why aren't You taking care of me?*

There in the dark, curled in a ball in the middle of her bed, Libby could think of only one word—the name of Jesus. As she repeated His name over and over, something within Libby changed.

As if she had just memorized the words from Annika's Bible, they came to her. "I have set the Lord always before me: because he is at my right hand, I will not be moved."

If I set the Lord before me, I will not be shaken!

Slowly Libby loosened the quilt. Outwardly nothing had changed, but inside Libby, everything was different.

In the next moment the man outside the door shifted his feet. After a time he started away. *Clump. Clump. Clump.* As Libby listened, the thud of heavy steps moved toward the stairs, then down to the boiler deck. For three or four minutes Libby listened, waiting to be sure he was gone.

Gathering the safe quilt around her, Libby slipped out of her bed. Without a sound she opened the door, looked both ways, and fled to her father's cabin.

When Pa swung wide his door, Libby knew she had

wakened him. After only a minute of listening to her, Pa asked, "Is the man still around?"

Libby shook her head. "I heard him leave. He went down the stairs to the boiler deck."

"Where he should be," Pa said. "That is, if he's a first-class passenger. Could you hear him walking around there?"

Again Libby shook her head, but Pa was already pulling on his captain's coat. "I'll take a look. Stay here till I come back."

When her father left, Libby kept the quilt around her. Huddled inside its warmth she listened. Finally Pa returned. He had found no sign of the man Libby described. "Why don't you stay here the rest of the night?" Pa asked.

"And tomorrow night too?"

"As long as you like. I hope we'll have this problem solved soon. But let's have a signal to rap on the wall between us."

"Two knocks, a space, two more knocks for *Come quick!*" Libby said.

Pa smiled. "And three knocks for *I love you, Libby!*"

As Pa sat down in his big rocking chair, Libby pulled up a footstool and sat down beside him. For a few minutes Pa rocked back and forth. Finally he spoke. "Libby, I don't like having you get caught in something so frightening. If this man is a friend of Dexter's, it goes back to one thing. The choices I make affect you."

As clearly as if it were yesterday, Libby remembered Pa standing up against Dexter and the man's threat to get even. Now, though she still felt scared, there was something Libby knew. "Pa, I don't want you to be any other way. I'm proud of you and what you stand for."

Reaching out, Pa hugged her. As he talked, he stroked

Libby's hair. "Sooner or later, all of us are put in a place where we have to decide what to do. We choose what is right, or we choose what is wrong."

"That's where the trouble begins." Libby was starting to catch on. "Once I choose to do what is right, I need to stand up for what I believe."

Pa's smile was slow and gentle. "You're growing up, Libby. You're learning to stand for something yourself."

Again he rocked without speaking, then asked, "Libby, did you notice what was going on tonight?"

Turning on her stool, Libby kept her gaze on Pa's face as she spoke. "I watched the men loading donnage and fuel— men I haven't seen before. They aren't our rousters or deck-hands. And they don't work on shore because they stayed on the *Christina*."

Pa's gaze was steady, and no change of expression gave away his thoughts. It reminded Libby of the way Caleb hid his feelings when something involved the safety of a fugitive slave. Then Libby remembered.

"Pa, I helped a woman come on board. She's going to have a baby. Maybe even tonight."

Pa's proud smile broke the tension both of them felt. "The owner of that sawmill, John Van Doorn, is a close friend of mine," Pa said. "When runaway slaves started swimming across the river, his sawmill was right in their path. John once told me that because of where he was located, he had to make a choice. Would he ignore what he believed? Or would he hide the outcasts? If he helped runaway slaves, he would be per-secuted as an abolitionist, a man who wanted to get rid of slavery."

"It's not fun having someone call you a name," Libby said.

"John knew that," Pa said. "So he asked the Lord what to do. When the Lord showed him, he did it. For years he's helped fugitives."

"Has God protected him?" Libby remembered her fear again.

"John doesn't do anything foolish. He must be very careful, or he wouldn't have lasted so long in this business. Yes, the Lord has given him protection. But I think John knows something I needed to learn. Being safe isn't having everything go right. What counts is knowing God's peace, even when life is hard."

Libby smiled. Yesterday she wouldn't have understood Pa's words. Now she did.

In the bright light of morning Libby woke up wondering where she was. At first she couldn't remember why she had made a bed of blankets on the floor of her father's cabin. Then it all came back.

For a moment Libby stroked the signal quilt she had brought with her. As the sunlight streamed through the windows, the dark red and blue pieces stood out, sharp and beautiful.

My safe quilt, Libby thought. Yet now the beautiful quilt would always remind her of more. *Lord, I thought You'd protect me from anything bad. I thought You'd keep scary things away from me. Instead, You were with me when I was scared.*

When Libby returned to her own room, she found that Caleb's grandmother had filled the pitcher on her washstand with water. Again Libby felt relieved that she could put on a dress. She found it tricky, but she was able to weave her long braid into her hair the way Annika had shown her.

Thursday, August 13, Libby thought as she started down the stairs for breakfast. *Only two days till Pa has to pay the loan in Galena.* Something bothered her.

"Caleb?" Libby asked as soon as she found him. "We'll soon reach the Lower Rapids, right?"

Steaming north, up the Mississippi River, boats faced two stretches of rapids. One of them, the Lower, or Des Moines Rapids, started at Keokuk, Iowa, near the place where the Des Moines River entered the Mississippi. Farther upstream was an eight-mile stretch called the Upper Rapids or the Rock Island Rapids.

"What if the water is low?" Libby asked.

"It will be low," Caleb said, offering no comfort at all. "It's August, remember?"

"What if we get hung up on the rocks?" Libby asked. A rock through a hull could cause a boat to sink within minutes. They would also be late in reaching Galena and making the loan payment. "After all our trouble, Pa might still lose the *Christina*."

"Let's hope it doesn't happen." Caleb's voice told Libby that he'd been wondering the same thing.

In Pa's cabin was a map of the Lower Rapids surveyed and charted by Lieutenant Robert E. Lee. In addition to being captain, Pa was licensed as a pilot and could take over for Fletcher, the trip pilot, at any time if he chose. Yet Pa always took on a rapids pilot—a local man who knew every rock in the dangerous stretch and every change in the river. Such pilots also knew the chutes—the passages or paths through which a boat could safely pass.

As Libby entered the large dining room for breakfast, she began her search for the man from the night before. Carefully she studied the face of every person in the room. Before long she noticed something else.

Last evening Annika had walked from the train with Aunt Vi between her and Pa. Once on board, Annika slipped away the moment she knew her room assignment. Libby had thought Annika was tired from traveling all day. Now Libby wondered about it.

According to custom, officers, not passengers, ate at the captain's table. Because they were relatives, Libby and Aunt Vi sat with Pa. Yet Annika had the choice of eating meals at the same place.

Now Libby saw Pa look around, searching for someone. She had a sneaking suspicion who that someone might be and finally spotted Annika at the end of the dining room, as far away from the captain's table as she could choose to sit.

At the end of the meal Pa started toward Annika, but the teacher hurried away before he reached her.

She's avoiding Pa, Libby thought. *She's making sure that not even Aunt Vi can accuse her of hunting for a husband.*

No longer did Libby wonder what was happening. She felt sure of one thing. *I caused trouble by what I said.*

Libby's heart was thumping so hard that she knew she had to do something about it. She headed straight for Annika's room.

Standing in the doorway, Libby waited until the teacher looked up. "I need to ask your forgiveness for what I said about marrying Pa," Libby said. "I'm sorry."

Annika smiled. "I forgive you, Libby. Now and then all of

us say things we're sorry about later."

"Thanks," Libby said. *And thanks for not making a big thing of it*, she thought. Libby started to leave.

But Annika spoke quickly. "I'm glad you're back with your father, Libby. He's very special to you, isn't he?"

From deep inside, Libby's pride in her pa welled up. "The most special person in the whole world."

"I heard what he told you about a never-give-up family," Annika said gently. "Even if—" The teacher stopped, and Libby couldn't read the look in her eyes.

After a moment Annika went on. "Libby, whenever you look at your safe quilt, bring my words to mind. No matter what happens between your father and me, I'm part of your never-give-up family."

Libby forced herself to smile. Secretly, though, she wasn't giving up. As she went out the door, Libby still hoped Pa and Annika would get married.

Only later did Libby wish she had asked Annika what she thought of Pa. *I wonder if Annika left family in Philadelphia.*

Once again Libby started searching for Dexter's friend the gambler.

CHAPTER 16

A Baby's Cry

One moment Libby wished she'd find the mysterious man. The next moment Libby hoped that she wouldn't.

Then from the front steps of the *Christina* she looked down on the main deck. On the starboard, or right side of the boat when facing the bow, she saw nothing out of the ordinary. On the port, or left side of the boat, six or seven men huddled around one man. His mustache spread wide and curled up at both ends.

With dread Libby felt as if she were reliving that awful moment on the train. This time Libby crept down the steps until she caught a good look at the man selling chances for jewelry. In the early morning light, Libby clearly saw his face. His hair was parted just off center and slicked down with something shiny.

Libby stared at the man. *Jordan and Peter are in danger again. If this man is here, so is Dexter. Now they're separate, so they don't call attention to themselves. When they need a job done, they'll be together.*

Libby's dread grew. *A job done. Catching Jordan, collecting the reward. Finding Peter, making good on Dexter's threat to get even. Perhaps even stealing from Pa again to keep him from making the payment.*

Quietly Libby edged back. Just as she was ready to step out of sight, the man glanced toward the stairs. For one instant Libby's gaze met his. The look in his eyes told Libby one thing. *He knows who I am. He knows I'm the captain's daughter.*

Slipping behind the wall next to the stairway, Libby broke into a run. When she found Pa in his cabin, he hurried to the main deck. By the time he got there, the men had scattered.

From the stairs Pa looked down at where they had been. "If you see the man again, tell me right away, Libby. On a family boat, I can stop him from selling chances—from using it as a way to pass counterfeit bills. If I catch him doing that on my boat, I can arrest him. But I can't arrest him for forging counterfeit bills without evidence."

"You need to find the press he uses?" Libby asked.

Pa nodded. "What does Peter know about the man?"

They found Peter leaning against the wall of the texas, as if to make sure no one could sneak up behind him. Libby's dog, Samson, was next to him. Seeing them there, Libby realized that the two had been together every moment since Peter came on board.

Sitting down beside him, Libby took his slate. Before she could write, Peter put his hand across it. "The gambler we saw on the train from Springfield is here on the boat. Is that what you wanted to say?"

Libby nodded. Taking the slate, Pa wrote, "What do you know about that man?"

"I think he's the one who helped Dexter escape from jail. His name is Slick. He forges counterfeit bills."

"You're sure?" Pa wrote.

"He visited Dexter in Galena," Peter answered. "One night when they didn't know I was there, I saw his press. They hid it in a secret place in Dexter's house."

"Do they know that you know?" Pa wrote again.

"That's one of the reasons Dexter wants to get me. At first he thought he'd use me to steal from you. He's angry because I stood up against him."

"Peter—" Pa began.

As though guessing what Pa was going to say, Peter held up his hands. "I'll be okay," he said, "if Libby doesn't care that Samson stays with me."

At the sound of his name, the big Newfoundland moved even closer to Peter. "See how much he likes me?" Peter scratched behind Samson's ears. "God and Caleb and Samson will take care of me."

"In that order?" Pa wrote.

Peter grinned. "In that order. It will help you find Slick if you know he uses special oil on his hair. You can smell it, even in the dark."

On that hot August morning, Libby felt a coldness that had nothing to do with the weather. *Peter meant it when he said he knew how to hide from Dexter. Has he also learned to hide from Slick?*

At Keokuk, Iowa, they came to the south end of the Des Moines Rapids. Pa took one look at the water and said, "It's really low. I've got too much freight for Muscatine. We'll have to lighten her up."

Wagons with teams of horses stood along the riverfront.

All hands pitched in, unloading freight until the *Christina* rode high enough for Pa's satisfaction. Then Caleb, Peter, and Samson climbed onto a wagon and rode overland. The *Christina* would meet the wagons at the upper end of the rapids.

Before leaving Keokuk, Pa took on a local pilot who knew the Des Moines Rapids. They were partway through the eleven-mile stretch when Pa found Libby on the hurricane deck.

"Libby, Gran has been watching the woman you brought on board. Sadie is about to have her baby."

"Oh good!" Libby exclaimed. "I knew she would, now that she's in a safe place."

Then Libby saw the look on Pa's face. Beads of perspiration formed a line along his upper lip. Sweat stood out on his forehead and streaked his cheeks. Deep in the cargo area where no air reached, it was very warm. Yet Libby sensed it was more.

"You've delivered babies before," she said. "You've told me about them."

"I went to see Sadie, but there's something wrong. I need a doctor. Go talk to the clerk. Check the passenger list. See if we have a doctor on board."

At the clerk's office Libby learned the worst. Though a doctor could usually be found among three hundred passengers, there was none listed for this trip. Sick at heart, Libby started back to tell Pa the bad news. On the way there she ran into Annika.

"What's wrong?" the teacher asked the minute she saw Libby's face.

Explaining quickly, Libby said, "Pa says Sadie needs a doctor. He doesn't know what to do."

"I'll take a look," Annika said. "Just give me a minute."

Annika hurried to her room and returned with a small black bag. "Is there another woman who can help me?"

"Gran—Caleb's grandmother—is already there. I'll show you the way."

When they reached the main deck, Libby led Annika through the door into the cargo area. In spite of the daylight outside, the room was dark. For Sadie's sake Pa had ordered that all doors be kept closed.

At the front of the cargo area Libby lit the lantern. Annika followed her back into the hiding place between boxes of freight. They found Gran kneeling on the floor next to Sadie.

At the sight of Annika relief flooded Gran's face. Standing up, she walked outside the hiding place to whisper to Annika. "The baby isn't coming the way it should."

To Libby Gran said, "Get us hot water. Boiling water."

Without a second thought Libby turned to obey. Leaving the lantern with Annika, she started back toward the door at the front of the cargo area. She had gone only a few steps when she heard a noise.

Stopping in her tracks, she listened. *Can it be a cat?* Then Libby knew it was a human sound. Someone was there in the darkness.

Libby swallowed hard. In her worry about Sadie, she had thrown caution to the wind. While passing from the bottom of the stairs to the cargo area, she had forgotten to look around. *I didn't make sure that no one watched. I led Annika straight here. And someone else!*

Rooted to the spot, Libby strained to hear. This time she heard a soft, muffled sound. *Who is it?*

She could only hope it was a deckhand. *But none of the crew would be so secretive.*

Then, waiting in the dark, Libby heard another sound. A dull thud coming closer. The sound of boots with a higher heel. *Clump. Clump. Clump.*

Her fear growing, Libby thought back. *Last night outside my room. The man on the deck. Walking round and round with that dreadful thump.* Libby felt sure that man was the gambler Peter described as Slick. But how could she know?

In the next instant Libby remembered Sadie. *What if she makes a noise? What if her baby is born?*

"*Babies need to cry at birth,*" Pa had said. "*It fills their lungs with air. Helps them live.*"

In the darkness Libby heard the scratch of a match. A flame flickered, then a candle moved closer and closer. Soon the man would spot the opening between tall piles of freight. He would see into the hidden room. He would pounce upon Sadie, a fugitive slave.

With dread Libby knew the worst. *I told Sadie she'd be safe. If the wrong person finds her, she'll be beaten, returned to slavery.*

As the man drew closer, Libby's panic grew. *Clump. Clump. Clump.*

Libby caught her breath. Only eight or ten feet behind her, Annika knelt on the floor, helping Sadie. *If Annika can help a woman have a baby, I can stop that man from finding Sadie!*

Boldly Libby stepped out. As the footsteps paused, the man held the candle so that she could not see his face.

Trying to hide the quaver in her voice, Libby spoke strongly. "This room is out of bounds for passengers. Only crew allowed in here."

From the darkness came an evil laugh. "And so, little lady, who are you?" Stretching out his arm, the man held the candle close to her face.

Libby stepped back from the flame but straightened to her full height. In that instant she had seen the slicked-down hair and the mustache curled up at both ends. She had smelled the strange perfume. *The man Peter calls Slick!*

"Sir, I am the captain's daughter," Libby answered. "My father would not take kindly to your having a candle here. Because of the danger of fire, no one uses a candle. Only certain crew members have the privilege of lighting a lantern."

Again Slick laughed. The sound of it tore through Libby's heart, but she stood her ground. "Now—leave at once."

"And what will you do if I don't?"

"I will call my father."

In the silence between them, Libby heard a gasp from the room-like space between piles of freight. *Sadie can't run. What if Slick finds Sadie?*

Desperate now, Libby remembered the night before. As if Annika and Gran were praying for her, Libby remembered this man's steps on the deck outside her room. Then she had cringed at the sound of his steps. Wrapped in her safe quilt she had cried out to Jesus. Now she knew one thing. *Jesus is the only One big enough to help.*

Silently Libby began to pray in the strong name of Jesus. *Help us, Jesus! Protect Sadie. Protect her baby.*

Then the light of Slick's candle reflected upward, and Libby saw the deep, hard lines in his face. The flickering flame threw evil-looking shadows across his face.

Yet when Libby spoke aloud, there was a sureness in her

voice that hadn't been there before. "Go," she said to Slick. "Go at once."

As if knowing that Libby hid a secret, Slick stood without moving. His cold eyes studied her face, as if testing her. But now Libby knew where her strength came from.

"If you don't leave here, my father will insist that you get off the boat."

As though an invisible hand reached out, twisting Slick around, he turned. With only one backward glance he stalked toward the door. *Clump. Clump. Clump.*

Libby felt sure he'd be back. She also felt sure he would bring Dexter.

CHAPTER 17

Rock Island Rapids

The moment Slick was gone, Libby flew to the door and closed it behind her. Then, feeling her way in the dark, she hurried back to the tucked-away area between the piles of freight.

"Annika," she whispered. "Can Sadie move?"

"I don't know," Annika said. "Her baby is almost here. What will we do if that man comes back?"

As much as she wanted Sadie's baby to be born, the thought of that first cry after birth filled Libby with panic. "Come," she whispered to Annika. "There's a secret room in the hold. If we get Sadie there, she and her baby will be safe."

Gran picked up the lantern. With Libby on one side and Annika on the other, they half carried, half dragged Sadie to the hidden entrance into the hold.

Kneeling down, Libby pushed aside the machine that hid the opening. The minute she swung up the trapdoor, Libby hurried down the ladder. Gran handed her the lantern, and Libby set it on the floor of the hull.

"It's only five feet down," Libby encouraged as she guided Sadie's feet onto the ladder.

Halfway down, Sadie moaned. Clinging to the rungs, she

stopped. But then, as if by supernatural strength, she kept on.

At the bottom of the ladder, Libby had the door open to the secret room that ran along the side of the boat. In the narrow passageway Sadie crawled forward, then dropped onto the boards placed across the beams.

"It's okay," Libby said as soon as Sadie's feet cleared the door. "You're safe now. You can have your baby. No one will be able to hear."

"Leave the lantern," Annika told Libby. "Try for hot water again. Hurry."

Racing against time, Libby started back up the ladder. As she knelt on the deck to set the hatch door in place, she heard a whimper, then the lusty wail of a newborn baby.

Leaning back on her heels, Libby smiled. Reaching out, she took Gran's hand and squeezed it. Sadie's baby was safe. Only those who wanted to help had heard that first cry.

As Libby went for water, she found Pa and told him about her close call with Slick. He promised to set a watch so that Dexter or Slick could not enter the hold.

A short time later, Libby lowered hot water into the small space next to the bottom of the ladder. Gran passed the water to Annika, then climbed out of the hold. In the low hiding place there was barely room for Annika to turn around.

As soon as she finished washing the baby, Annika let Libby climb down to see. On hands and knees, Libby crawled into the narrow room next to the great beams of the hull. In the light of the lantern Libby saw Sadie's shining eyes. "It's a girl!" she said proudly.

From her bed of quilts Sadie held up a small bundle. The newborn's eyes were closed, and her long dark lashes rested on rounded cheeks. Her thick hair was still wet and tightly curled.

"She is the most beautiful baby in the whole world!" Libby exclaimed.

"She should be," Sadie answered proudly. "The good Lord said, 'This child *will* be free.' And free she is!"

Smiling, Annika caught Libby's gaze. "Created equal," the teacher said softly. "It's a miracle, isn't it? Our Creator giving Sadie's baby life and liberty and the pursuit of happiness."

For some time Libby and Annika stayed there, sharing the miracle of that new life. Libby felt sure that Annika was enjoying this moment as much as she was.

Then Sadie raised herself up on one elbow and held out her child to Libby. "You wants to hold her?"

Libby had never held so small an infant. "If it's all right. If I won't hurt her."

The bundle was light in her arms. As Libby looked down, the baby opened her eyes and looked around.

"Your name, Libby. What does it stand for?" Sadie asked.

"Elizabeth," Libby told her. "It means 'Dedicated to God.' My ma and pa gave me to God."

"Ah!" A pleased sound filled Sadie's voice. "Then this child be Elizabeth—named after you. And named because I give her to God. I will tell this child how you helped her be born in freedom."

Long after Sadie fell asleep, Libby held the baby. Lightly she touched the small cheeks, feeling the soft skin. In wonder she watched the baby's tiny chest rise and fall with each breath.

"Elizabeth," Libby whispered in her ear. "Remember you're named after me. And your momma gave you to God!"

Then she could not see the baby, for tears blurred Libby's eyes.

Soon after she left the secret hiding place that sheltered Sadie and baby Elizabeth, Libby bumped into Aunt Vi.

"Well now," her aunt said. With a quick glance Vi took in Libby's dress and the braid pulled forward over her shoulder. "That certainly looks better. But a proper young lady would not perspire the way you do."

Libby opened her mouth, ready to tell her aunt that the narrow place that hid Sadie and her baby was small and hot. Then Libby remembered. In spite of all the excitement she felt about holding a newborn, she couldn't tell Aunt Vi. *She always misses out on the best things*, Libby decided.

As she reached her room high on the texas, Libby decided something else. *Sadie's baby is free, but I am not.*

Only five months before, Libby had come from living in a mansion to a room so small that her stiff skirts touched the bed on one side and the washstand on the other. *But I changed*, Libby thought. *I learned to handle it. Now I even like my room. Is that part of learning to be free?*

Deep inside, she still felt the hurt of her Aunt Vi wanting to give up on her. Yet now for the first time Libby knew what to do about it. *I can't change Auntie, but I can change the way I feel about her. Annika told me where to start.*

Libby wasn't sure how to say it, but the words finally came out. *Jesus, I forgive Aunt Vi for all the hurtful things she's said and done.*

When Libby finished praying, she felt relieved. At least she had made a start.

At the upper end of the Des Moines Rapids, the *Christina*

stopped long enough to let off the rapids pilot and reload
the freight hauled overland. As they put out into the river
once more, Libby felt grateful. In spite of low water, they had
steamed through the long chain of rocks without any problem.
Yet the unloading and loading again had cost precious hours.

"Only two days left," Libby said, but Pa assured her that if
all went well they would still get to Galena on time.

If all goes well, Libby told herself the next afternoon, one
day before Pa's four o'clock deadline for the money to be paid.

Three miles below the city of Rock Island, Illinois, the
Christina drew close to another landing. A new set of rapids
pilots waited where the Rock River flowed into the Mississippi
River.

Pa was delighted to see that his favorite pilot for the Upper
Rapids was there. "Philip Suiter was the first licensed rapids
pilot in this area," he told Libby as the *Christina* tied up. "Long
ago Philip brought his family to Illinois by building a boat and
taking it down the Ohio River. On a bad part of the trip, he lost
his seed for planting but not his three children. He lived in Illinois for a while, then moved to LeClaire, Iowa."

Libby had heard about Captain Suiter, the pioneer who
homesteaded a farm on the banks of the Mississippi. Yet Libby
had never been on board at a time when she could meet him.
Now she asked, "May I watch, Pa? From the pilothouse?"

Libby followed Captain Suiter and her father up the flights
of steps. As they entered the pilothouse, the boards on the front
side were completely open. Because rain or snow could build
up, cutting off the view, no glass was allowed directly in front
of where the pilot stood. Instead, four boards—two on the top
and two on the bottom—were hinged in such a way that they

could be open or nearly closed, depending on the weather.

On this hot August day, a strong wind caught the door into the pilothouse. Libby hung on, closing it carefully so the glass would not break. Sitting down on the bench next to the door, she watched every move that Captain Suiter made.

The pilot's face was shaved clean, but a white frizzy beard followed the line of his chin from ear to ear. Standing at one side of the great wheel, he spoke down the tube into the engine room, giving instructions.

With Pa and Fletcher, the trip pilot, Libby looked on as Captain Suiter put out into the river. Soon Libby saw the thirty- or forty-foot cliff at the south end of Rock Island. Deserted wooden buildings stood where the United States fort had once been located. Then, peering ahead, Libby saw the span of a railroad bridge that crossed the Mississippi.

The immense bridge was only a year old but had already provided much disagreement between steamboat men and the railroad. Built at a place where the current was strong, the opening was narrow and a dangerous obstacle for boats.

As Captain Suiter blew a whistle asking that the swing bridge be opened, Libby watched carefully. In spite of her confidence in the pilot, she felt relieved when they passed the huge bridge supports that endangered any boat that came too close.

The rapids were made up of rock outcroppings—a whole series of rock ledges. Between these ledges were narrow channels, or chutes, as the river people called them. The moment a pilot steered through one chute, he had to get his boat into position for the next. As though running an obstacle course, he backed and turned the boat, testing the current.

Slipping through each chute, Captain Suiter watched

for that slight change in the river—that unexpected rock that could tear out the bottom of a wood-hulled boat. Again Libby felt sure that he would take them safely through. Yet she couldn't help but think of stories she had heard. Stories about steamboats that struck a rock and sank to the bottom within minutes.

More than once the *Christina* met a steamboat coming down. Always the downriver boat had the right-of-way. With an exchange of whistles that signaled what he was doing, Captain Suiter gave way. At the first place where he could move just a bit out of the channel, he steered the *Christina* into slack water.

While they waited in the small pool of quiet water, Libby felt curious. "How did you learn to pilot the rapids?" she asked.

Turning, Captain Suiter offered a warm smile. "Do I have a cub pilot in the making? Come here. I'll show you."

With Libby standing next to the wheel, he pointed ahead. "See that large tree? And that high rock? Those are landmarks —places that tell me where I'll find rock ledges."

"How did you find your way through the first time?" Libby asked.

"I learned the rapids from two Indian friends," Captain Suiter told her. "They taught me about crosscurrents and where the chutes are."

As the *Christina* came alongside Campbell's Island, the pilot spoke again. "Current running mighty strong for this time of year."

Partway through the chute, Libby saw another boat coming downstream. With a quick exchange of whistles saying, "I'll get out of your way," Captain Suiter started for slack water.

"It's the *James Mason*," Pa said. "I hope Captain Jenks isn't up to his usual tricks."

Staying back of the wheel, Libby gazed at the other boat. While eating at the captain's table, she often heard talk about the hardheaded captain of the *James Mason*. Always he refused to pay the eight-dollar fee for a rapids pilot. More times than Libby could count, she had heard his words repeated by the men who knew every captain on the Upper Mississippi.

"I know those Rock Island Rapids as well as any rapids pilot," Captain Jenks would boast. "I'm not paying any pilot eight dollars just to take my boat through. I'll pilot it myself. I'll save the money and show them something to boot."

Even when the *Christina* slipped into a quiet pool below Duck Creek, Captain Suiter did not relax. Peering up the river, he watched the approach of the *James Mason*. Suddenly Captain Suiter exclaimed, "He's coming too fast!"

As the other boat started down the chute near Campbell's Island, Captain Suiter warned the pilot with four quick blasts of the whistle. "The current is too strong. It'll push him too fast!"

Ignoring the warning, the *James Mason* steamed on. By now the boat was close enough for Libby to see two men in the pilothouse.

"His own pilot is a good one," Pa said. "But they're having an argument."

As the larger of the two men took the wheel, Captain Suiter groaned. "His pilot would do better than Captain Jenks!"

Libby's father shook his head in disbelief. "I can hear Jenks now—hear him saying, 'I know those rocks, keep driving her. Give me the wheel. You sit on the bench, and I'll take her through.'"

As he peered ahead, Captain Suiter's eyes narrowed. "I don't know how he made it this far."

Again he blew four quick warning blasts. "He's booming through, hard and fast between the rocks. He'll make it through the chute. But just below the rocks he's got to come hard right to get over to the Iowa side."

Desperate now, Captain Suiter slapped his hand against the wheel. "He's going too fast—he'll never get her turned in time—"

A huge crash cut off his words. Like a leaf trembling in the wind, the *James Mason* shuddered along the length of its decks, then ground to a halt.

Libby's father moaned. "A rock caught them midship! A huge rock pierced the hull!"

∾ CHAPTER 18 ∾

Dangerous Passage

A woman's scream shattered the air. Babies wailed. Men shouted. Children cried for their parents. Through the broken rails at the end of the main deck, pigs jumped overboard and started swimming to shore. Above it all came the bawling of cows.

His face gray with worry, Pa began to pray. "Lord, have mercy! Have mercy on those people." Without a sound, Captain Suiter's lips moved, as if he was praying too.

In the pilothouse of the *James Mason*, Captain Jenks looked like a man wakened from a dream. As though not believing what had happened, he seemed unable to give orders. Far below on the main deck, passengers ran in every direction.

Then from the *James Mason* came the desperate whistle. Four quick blasts—the distress signal. On the *Christina*, Captain Suiter called down the speaking tube, giving orders to the engineer. "We're going up!"

As though trying to reach out to the other boat, Pa leaned forward. "They're taking on water," he said as the *James Mason* listed to one side.

Her terror growing, Libby spoke for the first time. "What if people can't swim?"

But Pa was too busy to answer. Leaning into the tube, he called to the engineer.

"Pumps! Every pump we have on board. Carpenter! Donnage to port. Prepare to board!"

Donnage? Then Libby remembered. The extra lumber a boat carried for repairs. *Can two crews stop the water from pouring in?*

Moments later the *Christina* steamed out of the slack water into the main channel. At one side of the great wheel, Captain Suiter stood with every muscle ready, every sense alert.

In spite of the emergency, he held the *Christina* at just the right speed. Weaving between the rock ledges, he found the narrow channel and stayed within the chute. Moving up slowly, he took care to not create a wake.

From the pilothouse Libby looked down on the *James Mason*. A large rock rose from the water near the front of the steamboat. The bow of the *James Mason* had just missed it. But farther back a different rock—a huge one—had pierced the hull midship.

People ran about, not knowing what to do. Panic filled their faces. Like a hand closing around her throat, Libby felt their fear.

On the main deck of the *James Mason*, crew members threw off the hatch covers. His box of tools in hand, the ship's carpenter leaped down into the hold. As though she were there to see, Libby imagined the water pouring past the rock through the open hole.

Moments later a cry rose up from the other boat. "Stuff the hole! Mattresses! Boards!"

Men and women raced into staterooms, pulled mattresses

off the beds, threw them over the railing. On the main deck, crew members grabbed them up and shoved them down the hatches.

Carrying pumps, deckhands ran to help. Racing against time, they threw open more hatches, dropped the long stem of the pumps through the hole. With one person on either side of a pump, they stood like men bowing to one another. Pushing up, down, up, down, they tried to keep the hold from filling up.

As the *Christina* drew close to the *James Mason*, Captain Suiter spoke into the tube. Moments later the engineer cut the *Christina*'s speed. Careful not to dislodge the other boat from the rock, Captain Suiter called down again. "Slowly, gently."

As the *Christina* came alongside, her crew threw out lines. The other crew caught and secured them. With the boats tied side by side, the bow of the *James Mason* lay alongside the stern of the *Christina*. Moving as with one thought, the *Christina*'s crew boarded the *James Mason*. Passing donnage from one ship to the other, they carried extra pumps to hatches, working alongside the other crew.

From the hold came another cry, "More mattresses!"

Libby sprang into action. Leaping down the steps from the pilothouse, she raced to her room. Flinging open the door, she pulled the mattress off her bed and dragged it across the hurricane deck.

"Watch out below!" she cried, then threw the mattress over the railing onto the deck of the other ship.

Again and again Libby ran into staterooms. Each time she threw a mattress onto the other boat, it vanished down a hatch. On her seventh or eighth trip to the side of the *James Mason*, Libby stopped dead in her tracks. *Something changed.*

For an instant she stood there, wondering what it was. The moment she knew, the fear she had felt disappeared, replaced by terror.

Forgetting the mattresses, Libby raced up the steps to the pilothouse. "Pa!" she cried. "The flag! The wind has shifted! It's coming from the northwest!"

It took only one look at the men in the pilothouse to know they had seen the same thing. Held by the point of the rock midship, the *James Mason* had already started to turn.

"If it comes off the rock, water will pour in like a flood!" Pa said.

Her panic growing, Libby peered down at the other boat. Men in the hold had felt the shift. Like gophers fleeing a hole, they scrambled from the hatches.

"We've got to keep that boat from drifting free!" Pa exclaimed. "If she drifts free, she'll sink us both!"

Leaning forward into the tube, Captain Suiter called down to the engineer. "I'll give you a rapid series of orders. Answer as quickly as you can."

His commands strong and clear, the pilot spoke without hesitation. "Come ahead easy on the starboard wheel. Come back easy on the port. Stop your starboard wheel. Stop your port wheel. Come back now strong on the port wheel."

With each order the boat responded. At last Captain Norstad said, "I think you got her under control. She's not swinging now."

Captain Suiter spoke into the tube. "Hold her steady."

Stepping to the window, Captain Norstad ordered his crew back down the hatch. Just then Libby noticed Caleb working with the men on the pumps.

"Get every male passenger working," Captain Norstad ordered. "Take every mattress you need from our rooms."

With new energy the pumpers moved up, down, up, down, trying to keep the boat from sinking. Then as Jordan took the place of a deckhand, Libby saw beyond him.

At the bow of the *James Mason* stood a young woman with a three- or four-year-old boy in her arms. In the wind her hair streamed away from her face. Seeing the panic in the woman's eyes, Libby felt a warning deep within.

She heard, Libby thought. *She heard someone say the boat will sink. Someone that scared will do most anything.*

Racing out of the pilothouse, Libby leaped down the steps. From one deck to the next she flew. On the main deck, she tore past Peter and Samson, then heard them follow her through the cargo space. As Libby reached the stern of the *Christina*, the woman teetered on the bow of the *James Mason*. Clinging to her child, she jumped into the water.

In the next instant Libby kicked off her shoes.

"I'll help you," Peter said. "I can swim!"

"No!" Libby exclaimed, then shook her head. "If I have trouble, get Caleb." Libby signed his name, then the signal for help.

With a running leap she jumped off the deck. As she surfaced Libby heard a splash from behind. *Samson!*

Libby knew he would grab her arm. *Just so he doesn't think he has to rescue me.*

Straight for the woman Libby swam. By the time Libby reached her, the woman had come back up, thrashing the water with one arm. Moments later she and her boy disappeared beneath the surface again.

Diving down, Libby grabbed the youngster from the

woman's arms, then fought her way up. As she surfaced, Samson was there. When Libby held out the child, the dog's soft mouth closed around the boy's arm. Carefully the dog held the child's head above water.

Moments later the woman came back up. For one instant Libby saw the terror in the woman's eyes. Desperate now, she swung her arm toward Libby's head.

Libby ducked, missing most of the blow. Dropping below the surface again, she stayed underwater to swim up behind the woman. In the next instant Libby brought her arm across the woman's chest and pulled her up to the surface. Still thrashing, the woman thought only of getting free.

"Stop it!" Libby ordered. "Let me help you!"

Instead, the woman pushed back a leg and kicked Libby. Treading water, Libby backed away but kept her grip. Soon she wondered how long she could hold on.

"Help!" Libby cried out. "Help!" The fear within her growing, she wondered if anyone would hear.

Still fighting, the woman twisted again. *She'll drown us both*, Libby thought. *I can't hang on!* Unwilling to give up, Libby clung to the woman with her last breath of strength.

Then Libby heard a splash in the water. Moments later she felt a hand reach out. A hand that stopped the woman's thrashing.

"Take Samson's tail," a voice said. Turning her head, Libby saw that it was Caleb.

Together they all swam for the *Christina*. At the stern, people reached out, finally seeing their need in all of the confusion.

Crew members knelt down, helping the woman and child

on board. Still panting, Libby hung on to the edge of the boat. Then it was her turn to receive help. Safe on deck at last, she sank down and leaned back against a large crate.

When Samson shook his body, water flew in all directions. His thick coat dripping, he nuzzled Libby's arm, then lay down beside her. Before long Caleb dropped down next to them.

By the time Libby caught her breath, men had stopped the flow of water into the *James Mason*. Deckhands still manned the pumps, but they had been able to nail boards across the mattresses to hold them in place.

When Captain Jenks boarded the *Christina*, Libby and Caleb hurried forward to listen. With a new look of humility, the captain of the *James Mason* asked Pa for a tow to the head of the rapids.

"Well—" Pa seemed to think about it. But Libby had no doubt what his final answer would be.

"You're a lot of extra weight for us to carry," Pa said, "and I'm in a hurry to get to Galena. In fact, I have no choice but to be there by four o'clock tomorrow."

"The people need to get ashore," Captain Jenks said.

"Yes, the people," Pa answered. "You should have thought about them in the first place. You could have lost a boat full of people. And perhaps you should take on a rapids pilot next time."

"Oh, I will," Captain Jenks answered, as though he had never considered any other option.

"If that's a promise—" Libby's father left the sentence hanging.

"It's a promise," the captain said.

"Then perhaps we can pour on extra steam," Pa replied.

"Perhaps we can tow you in. But have you noticed how much time we've lost?"

Pa tipped his head toward the west where the sun had dropped behind the trees. "You'll have to wait till first light tomorrow. No matter how much I want to get to Galena, it's not safe going through the rest of the rapids after sundown."

When Captain Jenks returned to his boat, Libby and Caleb went back to the *Christina*'s stern. As they sat down again, Libby realized that Caleb hadn't spoken a word since coming out of the water.

"Are they all right?" Libby asked about the woman and child they had rescued.

"Gran is taking care of them," Caleb said. "As soon as the woman settles down, they'll be okay."

When he said no more, Libby knew there was something really wrong. "What's bothering you?" she asked.

Caleb finally looked her in the eyes. "Libby, you scared me to death!" he exclaimed. "I was working on the *James Mason*. If I hadn't walked forward to their bow just then, I wouldn't have seen you at all."

Libby swallowed hard. She hated to admit how scared she'd been herself. Right now the woman's thrashing in the water was still too real.

But then Libby remembered Caleb's words after she was dragged to the police station. *"Don't you ever get upset?"* she had asked him. *"Only if it's worth it,"* Caleb told her with a self-satisfied grin. *"Just once,"* Libby had hissed, *"I would like to see you get nervous and upset and throw up."*

Now her voice was as innocent as she knew how to make it. "I really scared you?" She offered Caleb the smile she practiced on the boys in Chicago. "Was it worth getting upset?"

But Caleb ignored her teasing. "The first thing I saw was that woman hitting you across the head. You went under, and I didn't know if you'd ever come up again."

Caleb cleared his throat. "I thought I'd never get there in time. That I'd never find you in the water."

In that instant Libby turned serious. "Thanks, Caleb. I needed your help."

Caleb met her gaze. "And I care about what happens to you."

"I'm glad," Libby said softly. "You really care?"

"I really do."

"Good," Libby said aloud, but inside she felt much more.

"In fact," he said, "you're important to me."

"You think so?" This time it was Libby who could not look him in the eyes.

"You're a special person, Libby."

"I am?" More than once she had wondered what Caleb thought of her. He was so independent that it was hard to tell.

"You're almost as special as Samson."

Now Libby had no problem looking at Caleb. But Caleb kept on.

"When you dive off a boat to rescue someone, you need to ask for help."

"I did," Libby answered calmly, but her heart was still racing. Asking for help was a rule Pa taught her long ago. "I told Peter to get you."

"Peter? He didn't say a word. In fact, I haven't seen him at all."

"Uh-oh!" Libby said. "Where is he?"

"When did you see him last?"

"Just before I jumped in. I said, 'If I have trouble, get Caleb.' Then I remembered to sign your name. He didn't find you?"

Caleb looked worried now. "I was manning the pumps. The last you talked with Peter, he was standing on the edge of the deck? On the stern?"

"Right there." Libby pointed at the boards. "And Samson was right next to him." Just looking at the water that was growing darker by the moment made Libby feel sick.

Then her stomach turned over. "Last night Peter was afraid. He asked if he could have Samson with him. And Samson left him to follow me into the water!"

"Did you see anyone else?" Caleb asked.

"Like Dexter?" Libby shook her head. Then, like a bolt of lightning, her thoughts streaked out. "Dexter? Do you think— Oh no, Caleb! Not even Dexter would—"

"It would just take one push."

Libby stared at Caleb. "One push. And we would never know. No one could prove a thing!"

As the horror of it struck her, Libby moaned. "Oh, Caleb!"

Filled with terror, Libby jumped to her feet. "Peter!" she shouted without thinking. "Peter, where are you?"

~ CHAPTER 19 ~

The Hiding Place

Caleb jumped up, too, but he laid his hand on her arm. "Libby," he said as gently as she'd ever heard him. "Peter can't hear you."

For Libby it was the final blow. "I could call and call. He could be standing right here. And he wouldn't know!"

Tears ran down Libby's cheeks. "Peter wanted to come with me. He wanted to help, and I was afraid for him. If he had come—" Desperate now, Libby broke down sobbing.

But Caleb cut in. "Remember what he said? Is Peter really a good swimmer?"

"He wanted to help me rescue the woman. I didn't dare let him. I didn't know if he really could swim."

"But if he *is* a good swimmer—Libby, that changes everything!"

Suddenly Caleb's words reached Libby's frantic feelings. "We have to think," she said, trying to make herself calm. "If Peter has managed to stay alive so far—"

For the first time since knowing Peter was gone, Libby remembered to look around for Dexter. She lowered her voice. "If Peter is still alive, he must be in the water, right?"

"Some place where he could hide," Caleb said so quietly that Libby could barely hear him.

Now Caleb looked around. Neither Dexter nor his friend Slick were anywhere to be seen.

When Libby spoke again, only Caleb could hear. "Peter must be hidden, but hanging on to something. Are you thinking what I'm thinking?"

"Since the *Christina* hasn't moved, he must be hiding next to one of the paddle wheels," Caleb answered. "If the wheel turned, it would knock him in the head. That would be the end of him. But what if he was sure the *Christina* wasn't going to move for a while?"

"The housing—the wood framework outside the paddle wheel. It would hide him."

"That's where he is!" Caleb exclaimed. "It has to be! If he was pushed off right here, he's hanging on to the starboard paddle wheel."

"The wheel away from the *James Mason*," Libby said. "We've got to find him while we can still see."

Caleb's look was grim. "We've got to rescue him without Dexter or Slick seeing us."

On the deck behind the starboard wheel was a pen for whatever animals were transported each trip. Libby and Caleb slipped quietly between four mules, under the railing, and into the river.

The bottom edge of the wheel housing came close to the water without touching it. When they swam behind the housing, they found less light there than outside.

In the dim light the giant blades of the paddle wheel hung down into the water. Huge beams formed crosspieces that caught the water and propelled the boat forward. Caleb swam along one blade while Libby took the next.

Moment by moment it was growing darker. With it grew Libby's concern. *What if we can't see well enough to find Peter?*

She was almost ready to turn around when she saw him clinging to the innermost side of the paddle wheel. Libby could just barely make out his head. His face was turned away from her, but she could see his blond hair.

Filled with relief, Libby was ready to call Caleb, then remembered how sound carried on water. As she started swimming toward Peter, she thought of something else. *What if I scare him?*

Cautious now, Libby knew that if Peter turned, he would see her against the small amount of light left. Her face would be in darkness. *What if Peter thinks I'm Dexter and panics?*

Treading water, Libby started to pray. *Lord, I need your help again.*

Hanging on to the paddle wheel, she searched her mind for ideas. At last she remembered Peter at Annika's house. Peter leaning against the piano with his ear to the wood. Peter feeling the vibration of the music.

Still praying, Libby balled her right hand into a fist and pounded the crosspiece.

Suddenly Peter turned his head. "Libby?" His voice was little more than a whisper.

"Yes! Yes! Yes!" Libby pounded back.

"I'm here, Libby."

As she reached Peter, Libby saw that his entire body trembled. Whether with fear or cold, he shook so hard that he clung to the crosspiece with both hands. As Libby laid her hand on his arm, he took a deep breath but could not stop shaking.

When Caleb found them, he wrapped his arm around Peter's shoulder. Together Libby and Caleb helped Peter along the crosspiece until he reached the outer edge of the wheel. There Caleb put his hand on Peter's as though saying, "Wait."

If we could only wait for dark—real darkness, not just twilight, Libby thought, as Caleb swam outside the housing to take a look. Yet she knew they couldn't. Peter's teeth chattered, and his face looked pale.

Then Caleb returned. "We'll go back the way we came," he whispered to Libby. "When we get to the rail, you lift Peter from one side. I'll lift from the other."

When Caleb raised his arm above his head as though swimming, Peter's teeth chattered so hard he could not speak, but he nodded.

With one on either side of Peter, Libby and Caleb swam the short distance to the deck behind the paddle wheel. Caleb lifted the bottom rail, and he and Libby helped Peter up. When he rolled onto the deck, Libby and Caleb followed him.

The moment Caleb replaced the rail, they led Peter through the pen into a part of the cargo area near the kitchen. There in an out-of-the way corner he could be safely hidden from view.

"I'll get Peter some dry clothes," Caleb said.

"I'll tell Gran," Libby answered. "She'll bring him something warm to drink. Then I'll find Pa."

"Take care," Caleb warned.

"I will," Libby said. Never in her life had she meant a promise more.

When Libby left Gran, she crossed the cargo area and passed through the engine room on the port side of the *Chris-*

tina. Coming out on deck, she saw that the *Christina* was still lashed to the *James Mason*. In the gray light after sunset, Jordan manned one of the pumps. Then, as Libby started toward the *Christina*'s front deck, a man took Jordan's place.

Moments later Jordan stepped onto the *Christina*. Remembering that she needed to warn him about Dexter, Libby stopped.

Just then, near the bow, a man stood up. As though seeing the movement out of the corner of his eye, Jordan glanced that direction. In the next instant he started to run.

Dexter took one step toward Jordan, then seemed to have second thoughts.

Libby saw the look in Dexter's eyes. *He'll wait this time. He'll wait for some dark moment when Jordan is alone.*

Whirling around, Dexter melted into the crowd. But Jordan took no chances. Like a deer fleeing for its life, he zigzagged between people and freight. As Libby raced after him, Jordan passed through the doorway into the engine room. In the next breath he ran straight into Caleb.

As Caleb staggered backward, Libby slammed the door shut. "We saw Dexter!" she said.

"I need to leave this boat!" Jordan exclaimed. "If I don't, I'll get Libby's pa and everyone in trouble."

"Both you and Peter need to leave." Caleb told Jordan what had happened to Peter.

But now Libby remembered something else. "We've been so busy thinking about Dexter that we've forgotten Slick." Not only had the counterfeiter walked round and round the hurricane deck as if he was looking for someone, he had come into the cargo area, again searching for someone. "Where is he?"

Caleb shook his head. "With three hundred people and all this freight on board, there are countless places to hide. He might be watching us even now. But from where?"

In the dim light of the engine room, Jordan looked over his shoulder. "The Lord is telling me, 'Jordan, you get out of here fast.'"

"But the *James Mason* is stuck on a rock," Libby said. "And we're stuck with her. How can you get out of here?"

"I came in a barrel, and I'll go in a barrel," Jordan answered without a second thought. "But this time off the end of the boat."

Libby stared at him. "And Peter too?"

"And Peter too."

Just then, in the midst of everything else, Libby thought about the loan on the *Christina*. "At four o'clock tomorrow afternoon Pa's payment is due. And he's stuck in the rapids because he helped another boat!"

But Caleb knew what to do. "We'll take the money with us when we leave."

For the first time in hours Libby smiled. "*We*, you said. You and I will go with Jordan and Peter? We'll guide the barrels to shore?"

Caleb grinned. "And make the payment in Galena."

"Give me half an hour," Libby answered. "I'll try again to talk with Pa."

"Jordan, you're in charge of collecting food from Gran," Caleb said. "I'll get dry clothes for Peter."

From the engine room, Libby crossed the cargo room to leave by a different door. She was still in her dripping wet clothes when she found Pa in his cabin. "We're in trouble again," she said.

As Libby told how she and Caleb and Samson rescued the mother and child, Pa turned white. When she described what Dexter had done to Peter, Pa slammed his fist into the palm of his other hand. Finally he started pacing the floor.

"I put my most trusted men on to looking for Dexter and Slick," he said. "Yet the minute we were hung up with the accident, Dexter did his worst. I'll double the men who are watching for them."

"Jordan and Peter need to leave the *Christina*," Libby answered.

Pa sighed but he agreed. "Do all of you understand how to do it safely?" he asked when he heard their plan. "Hang on to the chine, the ridge on the bottom of the barrel. Don't fight the current. Swim with it to get to shore."

When Pa stretched out his arm to hug her, Libby knew they had his permission. "Tell Caleb I want to talk with him before you go. I'll pour on steam and follow you to Galena."

Pa shook his head. "I should have made it in plenty of time. But I won't take a chance on leaving those people on the *James Mason*. If something happened to them, I'd never forgive myself." Then Pa grinned. "I suppose you want to take the money with you."

Libby laughed. "Yes, Pa. We'd like to take the money with us."

When her father left to get the money from the safe, Libby hurried to her room. Feeling her way around in the dark, she dressed in the boys' shirt and overalls. With one quick jerk she pulled her braid from her hair and wrapped it in a cloth. As soon as she pushed the braid, a dress, and shoes into her knapsack, she was ready. But as Libby opened the door, she looked back.

A shaft of moonlight fell across the bed. As Libby stood there, her gaze followed the cream-colored path across the quilt. In that moment the quilt had greater meaning than ever before.

Bending down, Libby brushed her hand across it. Like a whisper on the night wind, she began to pray. *Jesus, I've always wanted to be safe, and I try hard to be careful. But there's something I finally know. What really counts is having You with me. That's what I want more than anything. So, Jesus, will You be with me—with us—no matter what?*

After a quick goodbye to Annika, Libby raced down the stairs. This time she remembered to take a roundabout way to the cargo area. After talking with Pa, Caleb rolled two empty barrels to the part of the cargo room closest to the stern.

When Caleb tipped the barrels on their sides, Jordan and Peter crawled in. Libby gave each of them a money belt. She handed Peter her knapsack, and Caleb gave his to Jordan.

Already Caleb had shown Peter the air hole and how to get out of the barrel by himself. Now Caleb told Libby what to do with the tight-fitting lid.

"Peter can kick out the lid, or you can pull it off," he said. "See the big air hole on the side? When your barrel floats steady, make sure the cork faces up. Signal Peter. He'll push it out."

When Caleb finished showing Libby, Caleb signed to Peter. "Ready?"

Peter grinned. "Ready." He was dressed in dry clothes now. No longer shivering, he just seemed eager to get going.

Caleb set the lid in place, then tested it to be sure Peter understood. When Caleb knocked twice on the barrel, Peter felt the vibration against his body and pushed out the cork. When

Caleb knocked three times, Peter pushed out the lid.

This time it was Caleb who grinned his approval. Once again he set the lid in place.

"Don't fight the current," he now warned Libby as Pa had. "Let it carry you downstream, but keep swimming toward the Iowa shore. We'll walk upriver from there."

The minute Jordan was ready, Caleb and Libby rolled the barrels out the door onto the narrow deck at the stern. The water was only a foot or so below the deck. For a moment they waited, letting their eyes grow used to the darkness. Then Libby rolled Peter's barrel off the edge.

CHAPTER 20

Galena Surprise

With a gentle splash Peter's barrel landed in the river. Slipping in after it, Libby swam to the side of the barrel away from the *Christina*. The one-inch chine, or ridge, on the bottom of the barrel gave a good handhold, and she hung on.

A moment later Jordan's barrel splashed down. As soon as Caleb slipped off the stern, he also took the side of the barrel away from the boat.

Then Libby felt the current against her legs and was glad that Pa and Caleb had told her not to fight it. Using one arm to swim and kicking to propel herself, she let the current carry her.

Can anyone see us? Libby wondered. With dread she thought of Dexter and Slick and felt glad for the darkness. *Does it look like the barrels fell overboard? That they're just floating down the river?*

As the barrels drifted away from the boat, Libby looked up. Pa stood on the hurricane deck, watching them. She wanted to wave to him, to tell him how scared she felt. But then without being told, she knew. Pa was praying for them. She could sense the help it gave.

When the barrel drifted well with the current, Libby turned it so the hole in the side faced the sky. Knocking twice, she waited for Peter, then caught the cork as he pushed it out. Shoving the cork into a pocket, Libby swam on.

So far so good, she thought, feeling pleased with how they were doing.

Farther and farther from the *Christina* they drifted. With each foot and yard of distance Libby felt better. *We're leaving Dexter and Slick behind!*

Often Libby glanced at Caleb. With the moonlight making a path across the water, he was easy to keep in sight. Bobbing now above the rocks, moving more swiftly where the current was strong, they kept the barrels fairly close together.

Once, Libby scraped against a boulder. Another time she caught her breath in an eddy that flung them around. Finally, some distance downstream, she stretched her legs and felt bottom. Still guiding the barrel, she stood up and pushed it to shore.

"We got away!" she exclaimed as she and Caleb rolled their barrels up the bank. "We got clean away!" Even now it seemed too good to be true.

Three times she rapped on the barrel, and Peter kicked off the lid. When he and Jordan climbed out, they rolled the barrels farther up on shore, lodging them behind a clump of bushes. Then they set out, following the river to find their way to LeClaire, Iowa.

Inside their barrels, Jordan and Peter had stayed dry. At first Libby's wet clothes felt cold and clammy. Then as they walked, the shirt and overalls began to feel steamy with heat.

In the half-light before dawn, Libby looked ahead and saw

the spreading arms of a great elm. "The Green Tree Hotel!" she exclaimed. From earlier trips up the river she remembered the famous Rock Elm.

"Folks say it's one hundred and twenty years old," Caleb told them.

Because of its position at the head of the Upper Rapids, most steamboats stopped in LeClaire, either before or after going through the dangerous stretch of water. River people from St. Paul to New Orleans knew about the Green Tree. Under its branches the rapids pilots waited, talked together, ate, and slept until a steamboat came along and needed a pilot.

Sawmills lined the LeClaire shoreline. Near a shipbuilding company stood the great beams used to launch boats. At river's edge a number of steamboats were tied up.

One of them already had steam billowing from its tall stacks. While Caleb stopped to ask when it would leave, Libby, Jordan, and Peter went on to where the Green Tree arched its branches over a large area of sloping ground. Filled with relief, Libby dropped down on the big roots. Pulling off her high-top shoes, she wiggled her toes in the sand.

Dawn was breaking as she looked across the river. Seeing the welcome light, Libby felt hope. *Today we pay off Pa's loan!*

But now there was something more. Something inside Libby had started to change. Walking upstream she had found time to think. As she dangled her feet in the river, old memories seemed to wash away.

Then a soft tapping broke the early-morning quiet. Libby looked up. High on the nearby steamboat, the captain gently tapped his pipe against the bell.

On the main deck, the first mate came to attention. At

the top of the boat, the pilot left his bench for the great wheel. Libby pulled her feet from the water. "We need to hurry!"

Eager to go but wishing she didn't have to leave the Green Tree, she scrambled up. Shoes in hand, she led Jordan and Peter to the steamboat. Moments after they joined Caleb at the gangplank, the crew took in the lines.

"Eighty-five miles to go!" Caleb exclaimed as the steamboat headed upstream.

"Eight and a half hours," Libby answered. "We'll be in Galena by two-thirty."

For Peter it would be going back to a city in which he had lived for a time. For Jordan it would be more.

"I'll be seein' my family again!" he exclaimed. "Can you imagine what Momma and my brother and my sisters will say when they lay their eyes me? And Daddy—do you think my daddy is there?"

"You'll know soon." Caleb grinned at Jordan's excitement. "If all goes well, we'll have an hour and a half to find the man and pay the money for the *Christina*."

If all goes well, Libby thought.

In the woman's room she changed out of her wet clothes into her dress. Carefully she wove the braid into her hair the way Annika had shown her. Then, as her gaze met the brown eyes of the girl in the mirror, Libby decided there was something she needed to do. Now, while her thoughts still felt real, Libby wanted to write them down.

Going back out on deck, she looked for a place where she could be alone. At first Libby just sat there, feeling the cool wind on her face. Then she took out her drawing paper and a pencil. Instead of making a sketch she started a list.

Auntie Vi taught me to . . .
sew
draw
appreciate beauty
have good manners, especially when eating
do my best
keep learning—to grow in what I know
dress well

Libby smiled. *No wonder I don't like looking scruffy and dirty.*
When she finished the list, Libby felt better. *I don't feel hurt anymore,* she thought with surprise. Suddenly, like a song pushing up from within, Libby knew. *I don't have to be perfect! I just need to do what the Lord asks me to do.*

Then an even stranger thought entered Libby's mind. *Auntie never had any children. Maybe she tries to put all her love for children into me. No wonder she has to make sure I turn out right!*

At that Libby giggled. *I'd better not tell Auntie. Things will get even worse.*

Once more Libby looked at the list. *That day on the train Annika talked to me about God's love, and I pushed her away. Have I been doing the same thing to You, God? Have I pushed You away when You wanted to wrap Your arms of love around me?*

When the steamboat left the Mississippi and started up the Galena River, Libby stood with the boys near the bow. On the banks of the river, willow branches hung low. Clumps of birches grew here and there, the leaves still and limp in the August heat.

Galena, Libby thought with excitement. She looked forward to seeing the busy city again. Settled early because of the lead mines in the area, the town had become a legend.

After all they had been through to reach this point, Libby felt sure they had finally won. "We still have over an hour to find Mr. Thompson and pay off Pa's loan!" she said as they tied up in Galena. "The *Christina* is safe!"

From his years of living in the city, Peter knew exactly where to go. As they left the riverfront, he and Jordan led the way with Libby and Caleb close behind.

On a side street Peter suddenly stopped. In the next instant he turned, headed across the street, and slipped between two buildings. As the rest of them followed, Peter stepped deeper into the shadows. Pulling them in beside him, he pointed back.

Across the street two men stood as they did in the dark area between two buildings. Libby could see only their backs, but she would recognize them anywhere.

"Dexter and Slick!" Peter whispered.

Leading them again, he hurried through the narrow space to the back side of the buildings. When he turned to face them, Libby raised her hands palm up and shrugged to ask, "How did you know?"

"I smelled his hair oil," Peter said.

Libby couldn't believe that Dexter and Slick were really in Galena. "It's like living the same nightmare a hundred times! Will we ever get away from them? Will we ever get Pa's loan paid off?"

"Not till they're in jail," Jordan growled. "If they stop us now, they'll grab your daddy's money again."

"And we wouldn't be able to pay the loan on time." Libby felt sick. Then she felt angry. "How did they get here? We sneaked away in the dark of night. I was sure no one saw except Pa."

"Probably no one did," Caleb answered. "But if you were a crook and started wondering if you'd get caught on board, what would you do?"

For a moment Libby thought about it. "I'd lower the yawl at the end of the *Christina*. I'd row upstream in the slack water close to shore. Then I'd catch a boat in LeClaire the way we did."

"The way we did, except for one thing." Caleb pushed his blond hair out of his forehead. "They didn't have to drift downstream, then walk up."

Taking the slate, he wrote to Peter, "They were ahead of us."

"But they didn't see us," Peter answered. "Just now, as we started to pass them, they were looking a different way. When we walked down the gangplank, they probably didn't notice us because they expected us to come on the *Christina*."

Again Libby felt angry. Dexter's desire to get even frightened her. *How long will he keep trying to ruin Pa?*

Standing in the shelter of the building, Libby tried to think, but her ideas tumbled in every direction. With each moment that passed Libby felt more upset.

Then, in the midst of her turmoil, her worried thoughts fell away. Again she remembered the verse in Annika's Bible. "I have set the Lord always before me: because he is at my right hand, I will not be moved." *I will not be shaken!*

In that moment Libby straightened, standing tall against the building. She knew what to do.

"This time we ask God to help us win!" she said. "This time

we have Dexter and Slick where we want them—where the police can search Dexter's house and find Slick's press for making
counterfeit money."

Half writing, half signing, Caleb explained to Peter. When
Peter said, "Yes!" Caleb wrote, "We need a plan."

Peter's blue eyes shone with excitement. "I have a plan. We
get them to follow us."

Libby stared at him. "You're crazy!" she blurted out. "I'm
tired of running." But even as she wiped her hand across her
forehead, then made the sign for "Run away from here!" she
started to laugh. "That's what you mean, isn't it?"

Judging by the expression on his face, Peter guessed what
she said. Looking from Libby to Caleb to Jordan, Peter answered, "We can all run faster than two men, can't we? You
wait here. I'll be right back."

Staying behind the buildings that hid them from Dexter
and Slick, Libby, Caleb, and Jordan waited. When Peter returned, a satisfied grin lit his face.

"My friend, the city marshal, is on duty. Right now he's collecting some men to help him. We just bring Dexter and Slick
into their arms."

As soon as Peter told his plan, he, Libby, Caleb, and Jordan
hurried back to the Galena River. On the way there they were
careful to stay out of sight. When they reached the open area
along the water, they stood near the steamboats. Then, as if
they had just come into town, they headed toward the heart
of the city.

This time Peter led them along the street that Dexter and
Slick faced. Near the opening between the two buildings, Peter
crossed to the other side of the street. Walking slightly ahead,

he turned toward Libby, Caleb, and Jordan, as if talking to them. When they passed the place where the men hid, Peter glanced toward the shadows.

Almost at once he signed Dexter's name. Still walking at the same pace, Peter led the others onto Main Street. As they made the turn, Libby risked a quick look back. The two men were following them.

Along the winding street, new red-brick buildings stood tall and beautiful. On the side away from the river, a tall bluff rose straight up, directly behind the business places.

Around them the street was busy with people hurrying in and out of shops. With their thoughts wrapped up in their own errands, no one seemed to notice Peter. When he started walking faster, the men did too. Each time Peter picked up his pace, so did they.

Then from the boardwalk behind her, Libby heard the thud of footsteps moving faster. Her fear growing, she took another quick glance back. Dexter and Slick were catching up.

Moments later Peter looked around. As if seeing the men for the first time, he broke into a run.

Suddenly Dexter cried out as if he had been robbed. "Stop! Thieves!"

~ CHAPTER 21 ~

Annika's Safe Quilt

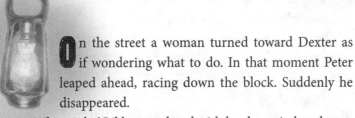

On the street a woman turned toward Dexter as if wondering what to do. In that moment Peter leaped ahead, racing down the block. Suddenly he disappeared.

Where is he? Libby wondered with her heart in her throat. After Dexter's threat to Peter's life, the possibility of his being caught filled Libby with panic.

Then, three buildings ahead, she saw Peter edge out from behind a tall man. On the boardwalk next to the street he darted between the people like a scared rabbit. Caleb followed next, then Jordan, with Libby running not far behind.

Filled with terror, she glanced back. Dexter was gaining on them now. As Slick pulled ahead, his boots thundered on the wooden walk.

Next to a tall brick building Peter disappeared once more. *Where is he?* Libby wondered again.

Then Caleb raced past an open doorway and disappeared. Soon after, Jordan vanished.

When Libby drew close to the doorway, she saw Peter standing in the opening, hidden by the wall. "Hurry!" he said and raced into the building.

As he ran through the store to the back, Libby followed close behind. There she found a flight of steps. Already Peter was partway up with Jordan ahead of him. At the top of the steps, Caleb looked down, waiting for Libby to catch up.

Up that flight of steps, then another, Libby raced. By the time she reached the third floor she was panting. Still running, Peter had taken the lead again. As the rest of them slowed down to see what to do, Peter hurried out a door.

A door? A door from the third floor?

But Libby had time for only that fleeting thought. From far beneath where she stood came heavy footsteps on the bottom step.

Again Libby hurried after the boys. When she passed through the third-floor doorway, Peter was still ahead, tearing across an iron bridge between the door and the street on the upper level. Again Libby glanced back. Dexter had reached the top of the stairs.

Libby's feet clattered on the bridge. Through the iron grating she looked to the ground three stories below. For an instant her knees felt weak. Gulping, she caught her breath and raced on.

Her side ached now from running so hard, but Libby kept on. Not far ahead, buildings stood close to the boardwalk. Beyond one of them was a large tree. Suddenly Peter swung left, disappearing around it.

Moments later Jordan vanished, then Caleb. When Libby followed, she ran headlong into the arms of the city marshal. Catching her, he whispered, "Stand aside."

As Libby obeyed, she saw that six or seven men waited nearby. When Dexter and Slick rounded the tree, the men surrounded them. Two men grabbed Slick. The city marshal caught Dexter and twisted his arms behind his back.

For a minute Dexter fought hard, trying to get free. Then, as he saw the men who stood guard, he stopped struggling. His face red with anger, Dexter glared at Peter. "I will *still* get even with you!"

Turning his back, Peter refused to look at Dexter. But Libby saw the pain in Peter's eyes. He didn't need to hear Dexter's words. Peter knew. As the city marshal and the other men led Dexter and Slick away, Peter's gaze followed them.

Just then Libby remembered Pa's loan. "What time is it?" she asked.

At the same moment Peter said, "Let's go!" Back along the upper street they hurried, then down a long, steep flight of steps to Main Street. There Peter pointed to one of the beautiful new brick buildings.

While Peter and Jordan waited, Libby and Caleb crossed the street. When the door opened to Libby's knock, a man invited them inside. In the hallway stood a tall grandfather clock. The hands pointed to ten minutes to four.

"Are you Mr. Thompson?" Libby asked. "I'm here for my father, Captain Nathaniel Norstad of the *Christina*."

"Come in, come in," the gentleman replied. He led them into a room with a large, highly polished desk. As Libby and Caleb counted out the bills, they laid them one by one on the desk. When they put down the last dollar of the amount owed, the grandfather clock struck four times.

When Mr. Thompson filled out a receipt he smiled. "That's the most interesting delivery of money I've ever seen. But it's all here." In large letters he wrote across the receipt: PAID IN FULL.

"Tell your father it's been a pleasure doing business with him. And with you."

When Libby smiled, the weight she had been feeling fell from her. "The *Christina* is free!" she exclaimed as she and Caleb went back outside. "Free, free, free!" She wanted to run, to shout, to tell the whole world.

Then she remembered Jordan's family. *Will this be a day of celebration for them? Where is Micah Parker now?*

As Caleb, Jordan, and Peter went to talk with the policemen about the counterfeit press in Dexter's house, Libby hurried through the streets. She could hardly wait to see Jordan's sister Serena again.

Jordan's mother worked for a steamboat captain whose wife had turned their mansion into a boardinghouse. Jordan's family lived across the yard in the upper half of the carriage house.

When Serena opened the door of their home, she took one look at Libby and whooped with surprise. "Where's that brother of mine?"

"Jordan is on his way," Libby told her. "Is your daddy home yet?"

Instead of answering, Serena giggled. Libby decided Serena had a secret she wasn't telling. But Libby knew she needed to squirm the information out of Serena.

"When your daddy comes home, it will be Jordan's birthday," Libby told her.

"His birthday?" Serena's dark brown eyes held a question. "How do you know?"

Quickly Libby told about the celebration of her fourteenth birthday on the bluff above Hannibal, Missouri. When she had asked Jordan his age, he didn't know. Nor did he know his own birthday.

Libby paused, wanting to be sure that Serena heard what she said. "That's when Jordan told me, 'I want my birthday to be the day I know my daddy is free.'"

Serena's eyes filled with laughter again. "Build up the fire, Libby," she said. "We is making a cake."

In spite of the August heat, Libby took kindling, then small pieces of split wood. Gradually she added larger pieces. By the time the heat of the cookstove made the kitchen unbearable, Serena had mixed all the ingredients for a cake.

"Are you keeping a secret from me?" Libby asked.

Serena wouldn't tell her, but when she slid the pan into the oven she winked at Libby.

The cake was baked and cooling by the time Caleb, Jordan, and Peter returned. Serena even had frosting all mixed and ready to spread.

Only then did Serena tell her younger brother, Zack, "You'd better go and see if Momma can come home."

Picking up the cake, Serena carried it outside, then down the steps into a small yard in back of the carriage house. On the ground she spread out a tablecloth, and all of them gathered around. Serena, Zack, and their little sister, Rose. Their momma and Jordan. Libby, Caleb, and Peter.

Leaning forward, Serena set the cake in the very center of the cloth. Then she and all the others began to sing. All the others except Jordan.

"Happy Birthday to *me*?" he asked when they finished. "Why do you think it's my birthday?"

It was Libby who told him. "You wanted your birthday to

be on the day you know your daddy is free."

"Free? How do you know my daddy is free? He can't be really free till he reaches his family."

Then, as if hiding from within, a light came to Jordan's face. Suddenly he leaped to his feet. "Daddy!" he called out. "Where you hiding?"

With a shout of laughter Micah Parker came around the corner of the carriage house.

"Daddy!" Jordan exclaimed again, as if unable to believe that all of his family was together.

Ah! Libby thought. *Jordan's daddy* has *been here for a while. Maybe even four or five days.*

Then Micah opened his arms, spreading them wide. "Come here, family!" he cried.

In one swoop Zack threw his arms around his daddy's waist. Following her brother, little Rose hugged her daddy's leg. As Micah reached out, circling Serena's shoulder, his arm caught Jordan in the hug. Micah's other arm closed around his wife.

With his family gathered to him, Micah wore a proud look that reminded Libby of Jordan. Lifting his head, Micah looked upward and spoke softly. "Thank You, Lord!"

Then a tear slid down his cheek. As other tears followed, Micah bowed his head. When he began to sob, his tears fell on Jordan's face.

When at last it was time to say goodbye to Jordan's never-give-up family, Libby, Caleb, and Peter started down the tree-shaded street.

"Do you think Pa is here yet?" Libby asked. Seeing the Parker family together made Libby feel lonesome for her own family.

As they came out in the open, Libby looked down the steep hill toward the Galena River. There beyond the tall brick buildings on Main Street, she saw the *Christina* tied up at the waterfront.

"Do you see her?" Libby asked proudly. She felt glad that she knew enough signs to tell Peter too. "Isn't she the most beautiful steamboat ever?"

But then Libby noticed something else. High on the hurricane deck a quilt hung from the railing. A quilt with a cream-colored background and dark red and blue pieces. From where she stood Libby could even see the paths created by colored pieces of cloth. The tracks of the Underground Railroad leading north.

Libby gasped. "My safe quilt! Annika must have taken it from my room!"

In a flash she remembered the teacher's words. *"Whenever you look at your safe quilt, bring my words to mind. No matter what happens between your pa and me, I'm part of your never-give-up family."*

No matter what happens . . . But now Libby wished with all her heart that the quilt meant more. *After I left, did Pa and Annika become friends?*

Catching up her skirts, Libby started to run. She ran straight toward the *Christina*.

**Don't miss the next
Freedom Seekers book,
The Fiddler's Secret!**

In the dark of night Libby Norstad wakes up. *It's quiet. Too quiet.* Then the rapid strokes of the ship's bell. Libby leaps to her feet. *What's wrong? What happened? Where's Pa?*

Minutes later out on deck, Libby hears the slap of paddle wheels against water. In the dense fog a steamboat whistles. A steamboat coming too fast, too close. Grabbing Annika's arm, Libby yanks her away from the railing. *Run!*

But out of the dark and the danger come the high notes of a gifted fiddler. Who is he? Why do his eyes seem to hold a secret? Why do both Jordan and Peter need protection?

Three suspects. Three directions from which danger seems to come. Can Libby, Caleb, Jordan, and Peter solve the mysteries heaped upon them? And what has happened to Annika? Will she be lost to the *Christina* family forever?

Study Guide

I want Peter to be safe," Libby thinks as she faces a sacrifice she dreads. *Even if he manages to hide from Dexter, my red hair could give Peter away. But do I really have to cut off my hair and dress like a scruffy boy?* Still—what had she told Pa? *I want a never-give-up family that believes in one another, sticks together even when it's hard.* Already Peter had started to feel like the younger brother she had always wanted. Holding up her hands, Libby made the sign for brother.

Hi Friends—What does it mean to stick together as a family, even when it's hard? And will Peter somehow manage to become a hero?

Let's Talk About . . . Words you might need
Find a dictionary and fill in the definitions:

safe house

depot

donnage

rapids

rapids pilot

narrow channels or chutes

slack water

crosscurrents

chine (as on barrel)

Let's Talk About . . . The story
To find something in the story, check the number (ch. 1) at the
end of the question. That means chaper 1. Look there until you
see another note (ch. 2, or 3, or 4) directing you to a different
chapter.

- When Dexter tried to teach Peter how to steal, what
  choice did Peter make? (ch. 2) How did that choice affect everything else Peter did?

- What sacrifice was especially difficult for Libby to make?
  Why was it so hard? (ch. 4)

- Why do some boys always think they aren't strong
  enough and some girls always think they aren't pretty or
  thin enough?

• In what ways do you value who you really are?

• How did the quilt at Annika's house offer a signal? (ch. 6)

• Why did Jordan quietly start singing?

• Caleb needed to remind Libby about one of the rules of the Underground Railroad. What did people working in the Railroad do to protect each other?

• Why did a fugitive or anyone working in the Underground Railroad need to keep thinking of new, creative ways to do things? Give examples. (ch. 8)

• Write a character description of either Annika or Pa. Whichever person you pick, describe what they did to help people. Include some of the encouraging things they said and did.

Let's Talk About . . . Making choices

• How has Libby learned to take responsibility for helping in whatever way she can? (ch. 8)

• What was Caleb's big news? What had he chosen to do? (ch. 10)

• Annika knew it was hard for Libby to pretend she was a boy in order to protect Peter. "But for now you must," Annika said, "and because you must, you will." If you need to make a choice that is really difficult, but you know it's right in God's sight, what will you do? (ch. 11)

• Why was Annika's quilt called a Jacob's ladder quilt? See
Genesis 28:10–22.

• What was God's promise to Jacob when he was afraid?
(v. 15.) How can that promise also help us?

• Why did Annika give Libby the quilt for a remembrance?
(ch. 12)

• Contrast Aunt Vi with Libby's mother. What did each of
them care about most?

• What made it hard for Libby to believe that her Aunt Vi
loved her? If you were Libby, would you feel the same
way? Why or why not?

• What did Annika want Libby to know at the end of her
terrible day?

• How does Annika help Libby understand how valuable
she is, both to God and to others?

Let's Talk About . . . Building dreams
• If you need to do something that is really difficult, yet
something that is right in God's sight, what choice will
you make?

- How might your difficult choices help you become the person you need to be for the dream God will lead you to build? (From an early age Caleb has wanted to be a newspaper reporter/editor. God called me to be a writer when I was nine and a half.) You don't have to know what God wants you to be when you're nine years old. But it's important to be open to His leading. Is He giving you an interest that might develop into a life-time vocation?

- What happened when Jordan delivered the money from his church to Mr. Jones? (ch. 14)

- Jordan also had the privilege of meeting Mr. Frederick Douglass. A former slave, he spoke out against slavery in the United States and became a highly respected, much-loved speaker in England. Learn more, and write about his life. Give reasons why Jordan would say, "When Mr. Douglass spoke, I saw the power of words. Good words help people. Good words change lives." (ch. 14)

- What can good words do for people? How can good words change lives?

- What do you believe will happen when Jordan learns to speak like Mr. Douglass? What does Jordan want to say?

- Why is a big dream worth having for every one of us?

- When Pa said, "Libby, the choices I make affect you," how did Libby answer? (ch. 15)

- "Sooner or later all of us are put in a place where we have to decide what to do," Pa said. "We choose what is right or we choose what is wrong." Libby feels sure that once she chooses to do what is right, she'll need to stand up for what she believes. Has this happened to you? Tell about it.

- What choice did the historic John Van Doorn need to make because of the location of his sawmill?

- How can the place and time in which we live make a difference in the kind of choices we need to make?

- How have the choices you've needed to make affected people you know?

- Libby wants to be safe. But Pa tells her, "Being safe isn't having everything go right. What counts is knowing God's peace, even when life is hard." What has happened that Libby now understands her father's words?

Let's Talk About . . . Forgiveness
- What very big honor did Sadie give to Libby? (ch.17) What does Sadie plan to tell her child?

- After Sadie's baby was born, Libby realized that the baby was free, but she herself was not. How did Libby pray, forgiving her Aunt Vi?

- Think of someone for whom you hold anger or hurt in your heart. What can you do to put those feelings behind you?

- How can you choose to pray in the name of Jesus, forgiving that person?

- Why was it important for Libby to also make a list of the good things Aunt Vi had taught her? (ch. 20)

- Guess what? It was a relief for Libby to realize she didn't have to be perfect! Why?

- Do you think that what Libby learned will forever change her attitude toward her aunt? Why or why not?

Let's Talk About . . . Being a never-give-up family

- Though she didn't want to do it, why did Libby decide to cut her hair?

- What are some funny things Libby did while pretending she was a boy?

- How does Caleb help Libby when she slips up and acts like a girl?

- When was Jordan's birthday? How was such a birthday gift a fulfillment of Jordan's dream?

- Think about Micah Parker opening his arms, saying, **"Come here, family."** How was the Parker family truly a never-give-up family?

Let's Write About Freedom . . . What is it?
- How have these four characters changed from the beginning of this series to this book? What were they like when you first met them? What are they like now?

Libby:

Caleb:

Jordan:

Peter:

- If you could be any character in the Freedom Seekers series, who would you like to be?

- Why?

- After reading about the Freedom Seekers, what do these words mean to you? Give examples from the novels or your own experience.

kindness

honesty

forgiveness

integrity

determination

never-give-up family

Digging Deeper . . . Wise words from a Freedom Seeker

- When in Springfield, Illinois, Peter met Abraham Lincoln, one of the greatest Freedom Seekers of all time. (ch. 5) Research Mr. Lincoln's life, his simple beginning, and his road to the White House.

- What qualities made President Lincoln one of our greatest American presidents?

- Search out the speeches of President Lincoln, the quotations for which he is famous. Talk about these words: "My concern is not whether God is on our side; my greatest concern is to be on God's side, for God is always right."

- While giving the Gettysburg Address, President Lincoln added the phrase "under God." Why is it important that we view our nation as being under God?

• During the Civil War President Lincoln would not al-
low the stars representing southern states to be removed
from the flag. If he had lived longer, what difference do
you think it might have made in the healing of wounds
between North and South? Give reasons for your answers.

• Think about starting a collection of helpful thoughts
that godly people have spoken or written. Put quotation
marks around the words, give the name of the person
you're quoting, and where you found those words. Put
them on 3 x 5 cards or a backed-up electronic file where
you can return to them often. In the same way, organize
Bible verses that are especially meaningful to you.

• Choose one of these helpful thoughts, and write about it.

**Will Jordan's family find a place of freedom where they
can live in safety and peace?**

**Join the Freedom Seekers a storm threatens their safety.
Can the *Christina* make it through the dangerous ice in
Lake Pepin? And where is Annika? Is she forever lost to the
never-give-up family?**

**Thanks for being my friends through books. I'll meet
you in the next Freedom Seekers novel . . . *The Fiddler's
Secret*!**

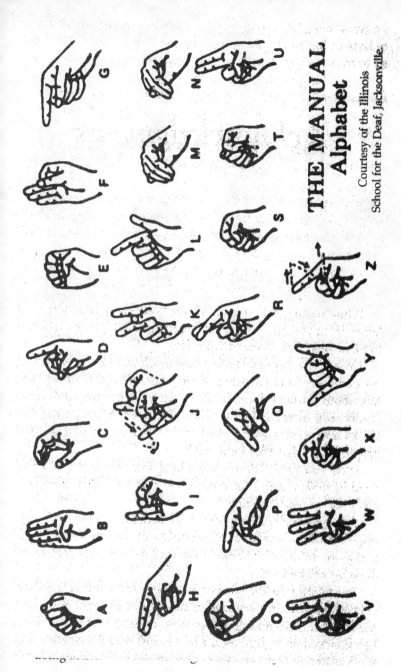

THE MANUAL Alphabet

Courtesy of the Illinois
School for the Deaf, Jacksonville.

A Few Words for Educators

Dear Parents and Educators,

The six novels in The Freedom Seekers series offer an excellent way to gain a national view of the political climate in 1857. In that critical period in American history, steamboats carried immigrants to newly opened land. Rivers were the highways of the time and the mighty Mississippi a well-traveled route. In spite of danger, injustice, and the possible loss of all they had, people of many faiths, rich and poor, slave or free, worked together for what they believed about the rights and freedoms of individuals. In life-or-death situations children, teens, and adults built the Underground Railroad.

As I returned to this series to write study guides, I was struck by the similarities between then and now. Though we live in an age of countless breakthroughs, some things have not changed—the need to value and uphold our American freedoms, the need to cherish human life, the need to stand for what we believe. **Even as we had overcomers then, we have The Freedom Seekers now.**

The Freedom Seekers series also offers tools for teaching topics that help our growth as individuals. Libby, Captain Norstad, Caleb, Jordan, Peter, and their friends face questions that are still crucial today:

- Who can I trust?
- What do I *really* care about?
- What does it mean to be a never-give-up family?
- How can I live my belief in the freedoms established by our founding fathers? See the Declaration of Independence. See also the Constitution of the United States, the first ten ammendments, known as the Bill of Rights, and also Amendments 13, 14, and 15.
- In what ways do I need to recognize the Lord's leading in both daily and life-or-death situations?
- What practical skills should I develop?
- Why do I need to put my faith in God?
- How can I live with biblical principles and values?
- How can I make choices based on those principles and values?
- And how can I encourage others to do the same?

The Freedom Seekers series weaves together fictional characters with carefully researched people who lived or were known in 1857. Each novel stands alone but is best read in sequence to see the growth of characters and relationships. Peter, a new character who is deaf—joins the *Christina* family in the fourth novel, *The Swindler's Treasure.* Annika, a new character, joins the *Christina* family in this book.

Prepare students for reading a novel by talking about the cover. With *Mysterious Signal* you might want to ask, Why is Libby in the water? What do you think has happened? What possible dangers could there be? Then encourage your students to just enjoy reading the story. If needed, they can take random notes to help them find details for later use, but ask them to wait with answering questions or doing activities. After reading a book through, students can return to it and glean added information to answer study questions or do other activities.

Each study guide gives you the ability to move through the questions and activities at a pace that is right for your students. For *Mysterious Signal* topics are organized in sections such as talking about the story, making choices, building dreams, forgiving others, and being a never-give-up family. The **Let's Write About Freedom** section gives student the opportunity to write about how characters have changed during the series. The **Digging Deeper: Wise words from a Freedom Seeker** section provides a way to learn more about President Lincoln. That sections also sugges starting a collection of helpful thoughts.

Your own love of reading may be one of your strongest motivators for encouraging others to read. That love and the discernment that follows will become an important gift you offer the children and young people you influence.

Whether you read these novels aloud, as a group, or your students read them individually, I hope that all of you enjoy them. May each of you also be blessed by growing deeper in your walk as a Freedom Seeker.

With warm regards,

Lois

Lois Walfrid Johnson

The Mysterious Signal Folks

FICTIONAL CHARACTERS

LIBBY NORSTAD: As she faces a big decision, Libby discovers how much it means to her to be a girl. What choice will she make about cutting her hair? Wearing scruffy boys' clothing? And why does she consider that choice in spite of all the ways her heart says no? Can this truly be part of what it means to be a never-give-up family?

CAPTAIN NATHANIEL NORSTAD: As owner of the *Christina*, Captain Norstad faces a deadline. Can he possibly pay off a loan that is due on August 15th? Because of ice damage, he had no choice but to take a loan to repair his steamboat. Then, because he stood firm and opposed a swindler's threat to an immigrant farmer, Captain Norstad faces the possible loss of all he has. Can Libby, Caleb, Jordan, and Peter overcome the obstacles in their path to bring the money to Galena and repay the loan before it's too late?

CALEB WHITNEY: Always thinking, Caleb tries to find a way to solve the problems he and the others face. When a train conductor refuses to correct a gambler's behavior, what can Caleb do? How can he protect Jordan and Peter from a cruel man who would harm both of them? And what steps will Caleb take toward reaching his goal of becoming a newspaper reporter?

RACHEL (GRAN) WHITNEY: As the chief pastry cook on the *Christina*, Gran is the call-on person to supply food to hungry fugitives. But how can this spunky, caring person do even more to give much-needed help to a young woman—a fugitive in hiding who will soon give birth?

JORDAN PARKER: Born into slavery and a much-sought-after fugitive, Jordan doesn't know his exact age, nor his birthday, but *does* know he has value and often wears a proud look. Humbled by the loss of money entrusted to him, Jordan longs to restore the faith of people in his church. Can he bring that money to the man who helps runaway slaves cross into Canada? And will Jordan be able to celebrate his birthday on the day he knows his father is free?

MICAH PARKER: Merciful, caring, tall, and strong, Micah has taught his son Jordan all that he knows about horses. With both of them having a big price on their heads, can they possibly reach Chicago safely?

HATTIE PARKER: Micah's wife, Jordan's mother, and a strong pray-er for her family.

   SERENA: Eleven years old with dimples in her smile and a warm heart.

   ZACK: Jordan's eight-year-old brother, who now has time to fish.

ROSE: Jordan's three-year-old sister, born during the time the roses bloom.

PETER JAMES CHRISTOPHERSON: Blond and blue-eyed, he looks surprisingly like a younger Caleb. Because he lost his hearing at the age of seven, Peter is able to speak. He explains: "I had brain fever when I was seven. My parents had it too. That's how they died. And that's why I'm deaf." But Peter not only knows sign language that he learned as a student at what is now called the Illinois School for the Deaf (Jacksonville), he's also quick to teach sign language to the others. But is Peter really a strong swimmer? And why does it become important that he can feel the vibrations of a piano?

ANNIKA BERG: Teacher in Bloomington, Illinois, for two years, formerly in Kentucky for a year, and Philadelphia before that. Blue eyes, black hair, tall, warm, compassionate, twenty-six years old. In spite of the dangers involved, she puts out a safe quilt. How does she become important to everyone who knows her, and especially to Libby?

VI THORNTON: Better known to Libby as her Auntie Vi. Will the terrible telegram announcing her dreaded visit give Libby an even more terrible day?

EDWARD DEXTER: A bitter, revengeful thief, always managing to do his worst. About five feet, ten inches tall, brown hair, blue eyes, wears expensive clothing. But according to both Peter and Libby, Dexter does not know how to dress. At the same time, he holds an important secret in Peter's life.

SLICK: A gambler with long, slender fingers and an illegal business, Slick has a wide mustache that curls up at both ends. His dark hair is parted nearly in the middle and slicked down againt his head with perfumed hair oil. He walks with a heavy thud because of higher than usual boot heels.

UNNAMED WALK-ONS: Springfield Underground Railroad conductor, Springfield police officer, conductor on the train to North Bloomington, shopkeeper, Galena policemen.

MARK CROON: Bloomington city marshal who is kinder than expected when questioning Libby.

SADIE: Young fugitive woman who responds to Libby's Underground Railroad quilt.

MR. FLETCHER: Capable, caring, long-time pilot on the *Christina*.

CAPTAIN JENKS: Stubborn, hard-headed captain of the *James Mason* who put others in danger by always refusing to pay the eight-dollar fee for a rapids pilot.

MR. THOMPSON: Galena man to whom Pa owes money.

SAMSON: Libby's Newfoundland dog who has not only proven to be a good rescue dog in water, but also offers comfort to Peter. Black coat with white patches on nose, muzzle, chest, and tips of toes.

HISTORIC CHARACTERS
This series is a place where you can bump into all kinds of famous people . . .

ABRAHAM LINCOLN: Remembered by Peter for his kindness and because of the way Mr. Lincoln carried important papers in his hat. Known by Annika for the excellent speech he gave in Bloomington, the city where the Illinois Republican party was organized. Known also as the city where Mr. Lincoln gave such a spellbinding speech that even reporters forgot to write it down. According to Annika, "People are calling it Mr. Lincoln's Lost Speech."

ALLAN PINKERTON: First American private eye, active in the Underground Railroad, and Irish founder of the Pinkerton Detective Agency. During this time he often rode the trains under contract by railroad companies to protect passengers from crime. A former cooper (barrel maker), Mr. Pinkerton is also a contact person for getting barrels.

JOHN JONES: A tailor and wealthy free black who used his home and abundance to provide for fugitives. He later wrote the paper that was largely responsible for getting the Black Laws of Illinois rescinded in 1865 and was one of the first elected officials of the city of Chicago. John Jones and Allan Pinkerton were friends.

JESSE FELL: Planted 12,000 trees in the Illinois city he valued.

HARRIET BISHOP: Early teacher in St. Paul, Minnesota, and friend of Annika's.

JOHN K. VAN DOORN: Owner of a large sawmill located on the bank of the Mississippi River, John Van Doorn provided an Underground Railroad link between Missouri and Illinois. When runaway slaves started swimming across the river, his sawmill was in their path. Unwilling to ignore what he believed, Van Doorn made a choice to help them.

ASA TURNER: Minister in Denmark, Iowa, who encouraged pastors coming to the frontier to marry women who were proud of wearing a jean dress.

AVERY TURNER: Asa Turner's brother. Farmer living five miles north of Quincy, Illinois, who put barrels along the Mississippi River to give fugitive swimmers a place to hide until it was safe to take the road to the Turner farm.

FREDERICK DOUGLASS: Former slave, gifted international speaker; the kind of person Jordan wants to become.

LT. ROBERT E. LEE: As General of the Confederate Army in the Civil War, General Lee ranks among the nation's greatest heroes. In this book he is known as the person who surveyed and charted the map of the Lower Rapids that hangs in Captain Norstad's office.

CAPTAIN PHILIP SUITER, LeClaire, Iowa: Pa's favorite licensed pilot for the Upper Rapids of the Mississippi River. Two of Captain Suiter's Indian friends taught him about crosscurrents and where the chutes were so that he could navigate the rapids safely.

* * * * * * * *

THE STEAMBOAT *CHRISTINA*: Name of the steamboat owned and operated by Libby's father and named after her mother. With the exception of the sidewheeler *Christina* and the *James Mason*, the steamboats in the FREEDOM SEEKERS series are historic.

THE STEAMBOAT *JAMES MASON*: Fictional steamboat owned by the hardheaded, fictional Captain Jenks.

TIME PERIOD: August 10—August 15, 1857.

Acknowledgments

Do you have a special code known only to you and your best friend? Or do you and a brother or sister have a mysterious signal for telling each other a secret?

Signals and codes are fun to think about, but for runaway slaves they sometimes meant the difference between life and death. Often fugitives had to decide whether they saw an offer of help and if it was safe to accept. Escaped slaves needed to be alert, quick thinking, and courageous.

If you and a friend used a signal, you would be able to agree on what it meant. In the Underground Railroad, strangers often gave signals to strangers. That meant the signals had to be very clear. Because most slaves weren't allowed to learn to read, written words could not be used. Fugitives were helped by symbols they could see or songs and code words they could hear.

Codes and signals often appeared to be something else. In *The Swindler's Treasure*, Dr. Thomas Brown set a lantern in his backyard. People thought the lantern gave Dr. Brown light for making nighttime house calls. In reality, a lighted lantern told fugitives, "It's safe to come up to this door."

One of the special ways slaves responded to a code word

came with Harriet Tubman's courageous rescues. Like the Israelite Moses, Harriet led her people out of bondage. A whisper passed from one slave to the next. *Moses! Moses is coming!* Those who wanted to flee were ready to go with her.

Their strong faith in the Lord carried slaves through extremely difficult times. Because they knew the Bible well, they were able to use its ideas in codes. These codes became part of their spirituals—call-and-answer songs sung to one another while working in the fields. In *Escape Into the Night*, Jordan sings "Let My People Go!" Because of their suffering, slaves understood the suffering of Israelites held in Pharaoh's bondage. The cry of the spiritual is their own longing for freedom: "Let my people go!"

"I got shoes, you got shoes, all God's children got shoes" was a protest song (*Race for Freedom*). Heaven represented a time when there would be no racial or social barriers. In God's presence there would be freedom. For Jordan and the people he represents, slavery has no part in the purpose of God.

With "Steal Away to Jesus" (*Midnight Rescue*), Jordan sings about the Lord in whom he believes. He expresses his faith in God's protection and tells his family, "Come! It's time to escape. Flee with me!"

The Bible gives us the story of "Jacob's Ladder." This spiritual and the Jacob's ladder quilt known in western Kentucky as the Underground Railroad pattern bring together two kinds of signals that remind us of the hope of freedom and lasting safety.

Because women aired their quilts by hanging them over a bush, railing, or clothesline, people who helped fugitives did the same. In addition to the Jacob's ladder design, other patterns are thought to be connected with the Underground Railroad. The Evening or North Star pattern showed the star that guided fugitives in their flight to safety (*Midnight Rescue*). In the usual log cabin quilt the red or yellow center symbolized a welcoming light or the warmth of a fire. A black center signaled, "It's safe here."

My gratitude to Dr. Raymond G. Dobard, professor in art history at Howard University, for his paper, "A Covenant in Cloth: The Visible and the Tangible in African-American Quilts," in the book, *Connecting Stitches: Quilts in Illinois Life*; to Howard Thurman for *Deep River and the Negro Spiritual Speaks of Life and Death*; to Joyce Grabinski of the West Des Moines Historical Society for her research; and to Julia Bloch of the American Quilt Study Group.

Five second graders—Amy Aillon, Marci Brown, Lyle Clason, Courtney Herrera, Kevlasha Humphrey—and their teacher, Kathleen Cook, at the Illinois School for the Deaf, Jacksonville, helped inspire the mysterious signal used in this book. Thank you for your gift of the lovely wall hanging quilted in the Jacob's ladder design. Kathy also answered my questions about sign language and my character Peter and spent long hours reading the manuscript.

Other students at the Illinois School for the Deaf—John Brand III, Kevin Healy, Dusty James, Michael Nesmith, Pearlene Theriot, and Joe Vieira—offered great ideas about what they would like to see Peter do. My gratitude to them and their teacher, Nancy Kelly-Jones, note taker Barb Ward, and interpreter Christine Good. Thanks also to Marene Mattern, educator aide at "Peter's School."

I am indebted to Joan Forney, superintendent, for permission to use the finger-spelling chart. Vocational instructor Dennis Daniel and teacher Kathleen Cook gave enormous effort toward helping with thepractical aspects of that chart. Thank you many times over!

Lois Wood, reference librarian at the Bloomington Public Library helped re-create the Bloomington-Normal, Illinois, area. The *Daily Pantagraph* published the *real* letter to the editor about gamblers who blocked an aisle on a railroad car. Other Illinois residents also helped in my research: H. Scott Wolfe, historical librarian of the Galena Public Library District; E. Cheryl Schnirring, curator of manuscripts, and other librarians at the Illinois State Historical Library; and Phil Germann, executive director, Historical Society of Quincy and Adams County.

Thanks also to the National Park service, U.S. Department of the Interior, for their restoration of Abraham Lincoln's home and the depot at which he spoke the memorable words that mean so much to us. On the morning of February 11, 1861, the Springfield Depot visited by Libby and her friends became an important part of American history. From the train platform President-elect Lincoln gave his farewell address to the city he loved.

The *James Mason* accident and Libby's visit to the Green Tree came from the inspiration of Captain Retired Dennis Trone, builder of the *Twilight* and the *Julia Belle Swain* and for twenty-four years captain of the *Julia Belle Swain*. With his piloting experience and strong sense of story, he brought to life the dangers and excitement of steamboating. Thanks, Captain Trone, for becoming a vital part of this book!

My gratitude also to Harry Alsman and Stephen G. Suiter

of LeClaire, Iowa. Joann Loete, whose husband, Al, is a sixth-generation descendant of Captain Philip Suiter, helped me learn about this gifted pioneer who profoundly influenced life in his area.

Settling on the bank of the Mississippi River, Mr. Suiter cleared a place in the forest to begin farming. In 1837 the family cabin was the site of the first school in LeClaire Township. Philip Suiter hired the teacher and provided the students--five of his own children. He and his wife, Hannah, and daughter, Mary Ann, were among eight members who established a church in LeClaire.

During 1864, the Mississippi reached the lowest water level known in its history. Captain Suiter made a mark on a rock ledge near his home that became the standard gauge for low water adopted by the government. He also passed on his love for the river to his sons and grandsons. Among LeClaire's many legendary river pilots were several Suiters, including a great-grandson of Philip.

Because of Dutch elm disease, the Green Tree enjoyed by Libby needed to be cut down in 1964. The bottom slab was twenty-one feet, six inches, and is on display at the Buffalo Bill Museum in LeClaire, Iowa.

Lucille Echols, Judy Werness, Mike Foss, and Nancy Lee Gauche gave me needed thoughts at just the right time. Sally Dale rescued Libby's long hair from an eternal wastebasket.

I am grateful for every person at Bethany House who played a part in bringing the first edition of these books to my readers. Special thanks to Rochelle Glöege, Natasha Sperling, and my out-of-house, long-time editor, Ron Klug, for their professional help, wisdom, and ongoing support. Working together, we've became a team. Bless you, Ron, Rochelle, and Natasha, for being both editors and friends.

Thank you to every person at Moody Publishers who has had a part in bringing out this new edition of the Freedom Seekers series: Deborah Keiser, Associate Publisher of River North, for her strong gifting, creative planning, and visionary leadership; Michele Forrider, Audience Development Manager, for day-to-day marketing and making connections with you, my audience; Brittany Biggs, Author Relations; Carolyn McDaniel, Page Compositor; Bailey Utecht, Editorial Assistant; Pam Pugh, General Project Editor, for her oversight, management, and working through the details that bring this book to completion. Thanks, also, to Artist Odessa Sawyer for giving us exciting art that keeps us asking, "What will happen next?"

As always, I cannot say enough about how much I appreciate the ideas, creativity, and encouragement given to me by my husband. Without you, Roy, this book would not have been written. With you it became a piece of writing I enjoyed.

Finally, thanks to you, my faithful readers. Your letters and emails come from all parts of the United States and over forty countries. My love and best wishes to each one of you.

[excerpt from *The Fiddler's Secret*]

~ CHAPTER 1 ~

Night of Fear

In the dark of night, Libby Norstad suddenly woke up. *Where am I?* She wondered as she struggled to think. *What woke me?*

A dream? A nightmare? Whatever the cause, Libby shivered with fear.

Soon after midnight her father's steamboat had left Galena, Illinois, heading up the Mississippi River. But now Libby felt no movement, heard no engines or slap of paddle wheels against the water.

It's quiet. Too quiet. Even the night air felt heavy and strange.

Then from near at hand the ship's bell broke the silence. As rapid strokes rang out, then stopped, Libby knew it was a signal.

What's wrong? she wondered. *What happened? Where's Pa?*

With a trembling heart, she leaped up and changed into her dress. As she stepped onto the deck outside her room, the cold fingers of fog seemed to clutch her.

Libby gasped. Without thinking, she stretched out her hands to feel the way. As she peered into the darkness, she could not see even eight feet ahead.

"Pa!" she cried in terror. "Where are you?"

Her hand against the outer wall of her room, Libby crept forward. When she reached her father's cabin at the front of the *Christina*, it was empty. Feeling as if she were sleepwalking, Libby turned around and started back.

Silly! she told herself, ashamed of her fear. *I'm on my father's boat. Why am I afraid?*

But the bell rang again, cutting through the ragged edges of her nerves. Forcing herself to be calm, she headed for the stairway.

In the four years after her mother's death, Libby had stayed with her aunt in a Chicago mansion. For the past five months Libby had been with her father. In that August of 1857, she was still learning to face the dangers of living on a steamboat.

I want to be strong, she thought. *But I just feel scared!*

When Libby reached the deck below, it was even darker. Usually filled with first-class passengers, the boiler deck was just above the large boilers that heated water and created steam to run the engines. With not one person in sight, the deck was strangely quiet. Libby had only one thought—to find Pa, her friend Caleb Whitney, or someone who would help her feel safe.

Instead, Libby found the railing and followed it toward the front of the boat. Through the murky darkness she saw someone standing at the bow. Libby's heart leaped with relief. *Annika Berg!*

The young woman's long black hair was pulled up to fall in loose curls at the back of her head. During the past week the teacher had helped Libby and her friends in a time of danger. Working with the Underground Railroad, the secret plan that helped slaves escape to freedom, Annika had given them a place to stay. In a few short days Libby had grown to love her.

As Libby took another step, Annika heard her and turned. "Come enjoy the view with me!"

Libby giggled. "What a view! Solid fog!" For the first time since waking up, she felt better.

Annika stood at the railing, peering down. "I've been trying to see if the ropes are out. We must be tied up along the riverbank. Right?"

Libby nodded. She could barely see the line, or rope, between the boat and the small willows along the river's west bank.

Annika faced her. "We're here because the pilot can't see, your father can't see—"

"Yes." Not wanting to talk about her fears, Libby tried to cut Annika off. But Libby's thoughts leaped on. *We're here so we don't run into a sandbar. So the sharp roots of a tree caught in the river bottom don't pierce our hull. So we don't run into another boat. Or another—*

"Are we far enough out of the channel?" Annika echoed Libby's thoughts. "Could a boat crash into us?"

Libby's hands knotted. It was her biggest fear. *If I don't admit it, maybe it won't happen.*

Now she wished it were Caleb talking to Annika. Though he and Libby were now the same age, Caleb would soon be fifteen. He also managed to answer questions better. A conductor for the Underground Railroad since the age of nine, Caleb had years of practice in being questioned by people not as nice as Annika.

The teacher met Libby's gaze. "If a captain thinks he needs to keep going—"

The ship's bell broke into her words. Then Libby remembered. On a steamboat tied up in fog, its crew rang the bell rapidly for five seconds out of every minute.

When the bell was quiet, Annika waited for Libby's answer. "The lines hold us as close to the shore as we can be without hurting the paddle wheel on this side," she said. "We can't get any farther out of the channel. We're long and wide, and the stern drifts out with the current."

"And a boat that doesn't wait for the fog to lift can run into us?" Annika's blue eyes were dark with concern. "Why doesn't your father just tell people to go on shore?"

In that moment Libby felt impatient with Annika's questions. Then Libby remembered that Annika was used to taking care of people—children in her classroom and fugitive slaves. Annika was used to thinking ahead.

Just the same, Libby felt she had to defend her father. Because of her, Annika and Pa had gotten off to a bad start. *I want Annika to think the best of him. To see Pa as a hero.*

"If we stay on the boat, there's a danger that something might happen," Libby said. "But we hope it won't. If we go on shore in the dark, it's pretty sure we won't like what we find."

"Such as?"

Libby shrugged. "I can't see what's here. I just know we're between towns, and there are islands in the river. If a riverboat captain finds a criminal on board and it's a long way to the next stop, the captain puts the man off on an island."

"Because it's a serious crime, and the captain has no choice?" Annika asked.

"If he knows his passengers might be harmed," Libby said.

Annika's voice was filled with respect. "I had no idea a riverboat captain has to deal with all that."

Libby smiled. *Now I'm getting somewhere*, she thought smugly. *I'll make sure Annika likes Pa. But I'll be clever this time.* From past experience Libby knew she had to be careful. Annika had already made it clear that she didn't want anyone to think she was looking for a husband.

"I don't know what else we'd find," Libby went on. "Some places there would be sink-down-deep mud, reeds, and tall grasses. Maybe floating bogs. Snakes."

"Snakes?"

"Copperheads. Timber rattlesnakes. This time of year, they live along the river bottoms."

"I see."

"Even in the fog." To Libby's surprise she already felt better. Annika could understand how Libby dreaded snakes and criminals and fog. *It would be nice having her around all the time.*

Now Libby knew just what to say. "Pa is a courageous man. A riverboat captain has to be very brave . . ."

Her eyes wide, Annika listened.

"And wise and good." Libby spoke quickly to make sure she got it all in. "He cares about his passengers. That's what makes him a good family man, a good choice for anyone who marries him."

Annika backed off. "Well," she said, "as long as I know we're in good hands, I'll leave you now."

Inwardly Libby groaned. *I did it again.* Libby wished she could bite off her tongue.

Instead she exclaimed, "No, don't go!" Already the fog

seemed to close around her. Having Annika there pushed aside Libby's fear. "I'll show you the lantern that tells other boats we're here."

Together they walked along the deck closest to the river channel. As they drew near the stern, the light of the lantern welcomed them. Yet the fog seemed even thicker than before.

"I wonder how far a pilot can see the light," Annika said.

Before she could answer, Libby heard the long, deep blast of a steamboat whistle. A whistle saying, "I'm coming! Get out of my way!"

Like a nightmare it was—a nightmare so real that Libby trembled. As the *Christina*'s bell rang without stopping, Libby shouted into the fog, "Watch out! We're here!"

But the deep whistle sounded again, closer now. Then Libby heard the slap of paddle wheels against water. With Annika at the rail beside her, Libby peered into the night.

Moments later a deckhand on the other boat called to his pilot. The front of the steamboat loomed up out of the fog. Frantically, Libby waved her arms. "We're here! Watch out! We're here!"

Now Libby saw the railing along an upper deck, the men standing as lookouts. As a deckhand called another warning, Libby's heart leaped with fear. "Don't run into us!"

But the steamboat whistle cut through her words, and Libby knew. *No one can hear a word I'm saying!*

Filled with panic, she grabbed Annika's arm and yanked her away from the railing. "Run!"

With Annika close behind, Libby raced to the other side of the boat. When Libby dropped down on her stomach, Annika fell to the deck beside her.

Hands over her head, face against the boards, Libby braced herself for the crash.

In that instant of waiting, she had one thought. *I don't want anything to happen to Annika!*

FICTION FROM MOODY PUBLISHERS

River North Fiction is here to provide quality fiction that will refresh and encourage you in your daily walk with God. We want to help readers know, love, and serve JESUS through the power of story.

Connect with us at www.rivernorthfiction.com

- ✔ Blog
- ✔ Newsletter
- ✔ Free Giveaways

- ✔ Behind the scenes look at writing fiction and publishing
- ✔ Book Club

MOODY
PUBLISHERS

www.MoodyPublishers.com